SHOULDER BONES

A collection of short stories about the macabre, femininity, and the southern childhood

MARY B. SELLERS

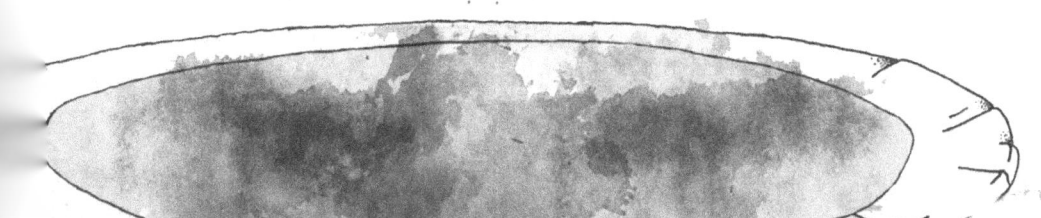

Shoulder Bones
A Collection of Short Stories about the Macabre,
Femininity, and the Southern Childhood
Text Copyright © 2014 Mary B. Sellers
Illustration Copyright © Cody Bass 2014, codybassdesign.com

Published by:
Blooming Twig Books
© 2014 Mary B. Sellers
All rights reserved

Manufactured in the United States of America

Cover and Interior Illustrations: Cody Bass

eBook: 978-1-61343-087-3
Paperback: 978-1-61343-088-0

First Edition

To the men in my life:
Daddy & Big John

Previously Published Material:

"Legba" in *Deep South Magazine*, January 2014
"She" in *Danse Macabre*, April 2014
"Light Language" in *Gingerbread House*, June, 2014
"Night Sounds" in *Mouse Tales Press*, October 2014
"The House Hunters" in *Danse Macabre Du Jour*,
October 2014

Cover credits: Cody Bass

"She laughed and danced with the
thought of death in her heart."

— Hans Christian Andersen,
The Little Mermaid

Stories

Little Ghosts: An Introduction

I remember trying so hard to move things with my eyes. I'd stare at a pencil for an hour, two, willing it to move a millimeter, in order to justify myself. I was in third grade then, convinced that if I discovered my telekinetic-tendencies, I'd be able to explain away a lot of the bothersome things about myself that I'd been happening upon.

One time, in second grade, I made my best friend agree to hold her antique dresser steady while I climbed atop it and jumped. I was sleeping over at her house — a house that any romantic would readily worship. There were nineteenth-century swords on the walls to the bathroom; robes from Asia hung unceremoniously in closets; an in-door heated pool that I, and every one of my friends, had convinced ourselves that the Loch Ness Monster frequented on her days off from Scottish celebrity status. I used an Office Depot broom, hitching it under my paisley shorts and gripping it until the muscles in my hands ached. As my feet launched themselves from the old wood, I heard a loud creak, a gasp from my friend, and a snigger from her older brother, who happened to be spying on us. I landed on her rug, fortunately, unscathed except for a brain-shaped bruise that appeared the next morning, decorating my thin bicep. It was, to my disappointment, the mark of mortality.

When I was five and in the bathtub, surrounded by my playthings — a mermaid with a mechanical tail, a few sea creatures, a *Toy Story* Bo-Peep shaped like a top — I looked up and saw a red-caped figure cross my doorway. I didn't shout, but nestled myself further into the warm water, cloaked in bubbles that popped on a whisper, and waited. It didn't come again for a while. When my mother quit her job when I was eight, I saw it again. It was rounding a corner in our new home — swift and dull but purposeful — the red was the color of dried blood.

I waited for these hooded figures for many years. I remember finally admitting it to my mother on the nightly walks we took when I was still young enough and smart enough to crave parental attention. I asked my whole-hearted questions without the faintest bit of embarrassment or censure. She told me that she'd also seen them long ago, but they had stopped coming because she grew older. I was twelve, then, and the possibility of growing too old was unfathomable.

The brightest memory I have of magic was when I was still living at my old house, young enough to be kept by my grandparents during the day; old enough to decipher fiction from fact. I was standing in front of my grandfather's truck, watching my mother hug her mother, thanking her, I'm sure, for keeping me while she and my Dad worked from eight a.m. to nine p.m.

And there she was — pumpkin orange, internally lit by something I'll never be able to wrap my head around. She was small — Barbie-sized, really. She zipped past my cherub nose and I know I gasped because I remember everyone turning to look at me. I was a child in the night, waiting for the warm tug of my mother's hand, and I saw a small, bright being a half-inch away from my face.

Now, there are still ghosts that laugh from the creeks in the park. There are the twilight hours on Sundays when everything is hazier and slower and more receptive to uncommon things. I see it in the way a cat smooths itself against my leg like a magnet. There is still a monster under my bed, meaning no harm, but curious, poking himself into my dreams like a troublesome pebble caught in my sandal. But when there's too much light, he leaves, forbidden by the day-to-day. In the daylight, there's only the unruly sock left, collecting its dust.

NIGHT SOUNDS

"**THEY'RE IN THE WALLS,**" my mother tells me, leaning in further. Her pale ear presses up against the dining room wall where a picture of my grandmother used to hang.

"How'd you know?"

"Don't you hear them? The creaking... listen... there's a moan."

I'm standing in the hallway in my pajamas, watching my mother go crazy. She's been hearing things for the past few weeks and I've been lying to my very busy father about it. He goes to work, then he goes to sleep. It's a cyclical thing that rarely pauses. And we stay up, listening, ignoring his dreams. There's a pull of loyalty towards her; she is my mother and I am her thirteen-year-old daughter. His vast and unknowable maleness excludes him.

In the shower, I find a dark hair on my nipple and tug at it until it comes free, rinsed down the drain like a dream. I turn the water up extra hot so that the steam looks like smoke, and I cry, again. Hotter tears than before.

In the morning, she doesn't wake up to fix me breakfast.

The sound machine she uses drones behind her closed door, muffled and angry-sounding. Noon comes, and she's still asleep, or still pretending to be, so I call my grandfather and ask him to take me to Sonic, the lone drive-in fast food place in our small, suburban town. I wait outside on the porch steps, watching sweat form in beads along my thighs, like a summer talisman, of sorts.

At the Drive-in I order a grilled cheese, medium fry, and a watermelon slushie. The woman who brings my food is centipede thin — brandy-colored hair, a tarnished face with wrinkles like tree rings around muddy eyes. Her hands are covered in scars; she is my mother's age. She smiles at me, calls me "honey," with a voice that is raw, withered. I take my drink and turn away in the seat, closing my eyes, listening to the rattle of change my grandfather finds in his sand-colored britches.

"How's your mother?" he asks on the way home, keeping his eyes straight ahead. I can see the whiskers in his ears.

He doesn't like going in much, because sometimes they don't get along. Ever since my grandmother died, they stare at each other with sharp, rattlesnake eyes. So he asks me how she is. And my father asks me how she is. And no one seems to want to ask her.

"She's fine," I say, something catching in my throat like a sob I can't shake, despite a mouthful of sugar.

It's summertime. The weather is sticky-hot like wet fingers climbing up and down my skin. There's a wasp guarding the garage door. I'm scared to pass. I want to lie in the sun, to work on the eighth-grade tan to premiere next month at my assigned locker, so I can get a boyfriend to take me to football games.

I press my ear against the back door, imagining this is how my mother feels, listening to the other end of things.

The wasp buzzes again. I hear him knocking himself into the carport ceiling. I'm afraid of small things.

My mother comes out of her room at three in the afternoon. She's in her bathrobe, and the blonde in her hair has grown out, betraying an unwashed, mahogany brunette. It's skunk-like, a zigzagging of color. I'm fascinated by her roots that look dark as dirt.

"I made coffee earlier," I say.

"Thanks, sweetheart," she says, brushing oily bangs out of her eyes.

"You didn't ever fix me lunch."

"Well, you got something, didn't you?"

"I got JB to pick me up and take me to Sonic. He gave me twenty dollars."

I hold up the bill JB — my grandfather — had given me. A bribe for silence or for the truth? I wasn't sure, but I took it just the same, folding it into my palm, and swallowing hard.

"I'll have to call him later," she says, working the corner of her mouth into a grin. She's gained so much weight in the past few months that I find it hard to look at her — all white legs, deeply veined, a rounded belly. I wonder if my father loves her anymore.

My mother is taking a walk. I'm on the old desktop, fiddling around with HTML and CSS codes — a hobby I'd picked up in seventh-grade computer class, when I hadn't picked up any friends. I like creating things with pixels — zooming up close to 200% and marking each square with a specific shade of #C62020 and #07598C like some sort of weird, planned acne.

Eventually, I get up to look in the pantry for cereal, and I see my mother lying on the pavement, staring up into the wide expanse of faint blue stars appearing like dusk's chaperone. Her body is spread out as if she's trying to make a snow angel in the cement. I walk outside, barefoot.

"Mom, what're you doing?" My voice sounds strange and tinny in this twilight hour of deep, summer golds and katydid songs.

I know what she's doing. She's trying to find something that's already left her a while back, taking her sanity with it. She doesn't move so I go down the brick steps and walk into the street. I nudge her with my big toe.

"Go back inside," she says, caught in a dream I cannot see.

"No, get up. The neighbors are gonna see," I say impatiently.

"They can't see me," she says, smiling with small teeth that hold a secret. I want to smash it.

"Yes, they can."

I start pulling her up, grabbing at her arm roughly, and she lets it hang loose like a dead thing. She finally gets up and her eyes are black matte. There is nothing in them — just inkwells that have gone and dried up. I slap her, then, with all of my childish strength, and see the pink outline of my handprint on her shoulder. She doesn't even flinch, but passes me and goes into the house, humming some off-key tune.

I listen to my mother's soft steps late into the night. My father came home late, tired and suspicious. She's everywhere at once — a collective thing that thinks the air conditioning tap is a friendly ghost; the katydids outside are a call to arms; that I'm just another shadow. There's something to be said for losing yourself.

Maybe I'll tell my father tomorrow.

THE RISING

I STAYED IN SPACE.

I crouched down, feeling the trampoline's sun-warmed surface against the bottoms of my sock feet. I pushed forwards, my ninety-eight pounds straight down into the springy surface, then straining, up and up and up, until it was just the air — merely the rocketing crash and thrill of air — but I didn't come down.

Three policemen stared up at me. I imagined them thinking: *it's a bird, a plane, a... girl?* Their mouths were crooked open, and their eyes fixed on the space between the trampoline and my sock feet. There, under where my toes dangled, was the unexplainable patch of air.

My mother stood folded into my father's arm, so small, hands clasped between her breasts as if in prayer. The sun combed copper into her hair. She shaded her eyes with a limp right hand that curved her face into a perfect oval. I tried to catch her eye, but it seemed no one wanted to catch mine. My feet got all the attention.

"How long she's been like this?" asked an officer with a pencil-thin moustache that etched accidental authority into his cheekbones. He stood like an amateur actor.

"A half hour," my father replied, clutching my mother's shoulder, waving his head faintly as if to brush the impossibility of it from his words.

"And... no other incidents... like this?" the cop asked, shifting both hands to where I assumed his hips used to be. As if getting stuck in air was a relatively normal activity for any thirteen-year-old.

"What do you think?" bristled my father, unwrapping himself from my mother like a daddy longlegs, hands thumping the sides of his hips, face in a storm scowl. My mother looked even smaller — a space apart from him.

"I jumped," I offered. "I'd been jumping for hours and then...." I gestured to my dangling lower half and shrugged.

Everyone met my gaze for the first time. Somehow, I still managed to be an afterthought.

"You know, I can still hear properly," I said, a little angry. Their eyes itched like ants on my skin.

"We need to call a specialist in... matters such as these," said the cop.

"Oh, right, there's an expert on little girls getting...." My father gestured to me in a vague, see-what-she's-doing arm swipe.

"What else do you suggest, Mister? We've already tried the firemen and the ladder. Wouldn't budge."

The firemen had just loaded up and left, drawing a curious jumble of onlookers, which the policemen glared away. After tugging at my limbs for a good fifteen minutes, they'd made me feel like a tacked-on picture frame that refused to unfasten itself from a wall. My shoulder ached from where my socket had been strained by their rough, gloved hands. They called me a damsel; I called them assholes. They were surprised by my thirteen-year-old vocabulary. My mother looked shocked.

There were still a few onlookers crouched behind my mother's azalea bushes, and the large magnolia in our front yard — mainly housewives in mauves and sea foam house robes, craning their sagging, white necks like lady chickens in a coop. *Step on up, ladies, squawk squawk squawk,* I thought, knowing for a fact that the news had probably already spread to WXKG 300.

The only thing that ever happened in our neighborhood was the annual block party. Where, without fail, Mr. Dempsy, the resident bachelor, got drunk on his vodka coke. He tried to hit on the various eager-yet-coy-in-curlers forty-somethings, whose husbands had better things to do than eat mild cheddar cheese straws and sip on bad gin in the August heat. After a couple, he always let me slip a bit of booze into my own paisley print paper cup, giving me a wink, and proceeding to gruffly punch me in the shoulder. One time, after taking me to his car to get more booze, he invited me in the back seat.

"You're so small," he said, staring resolutely at the polyester V-neck I wore. I felt the soft swell of breasts rise with my shallow, nervous breaths, and identified that feeling as womanhood.

"Thirteen-year-olds usually are," I said, instantly regretting calling attention to my age. I leaned in and kissed him how I'd seen Angelina Jolie do in movies. I angled my head too much, and when our closed lips met, a strand of my ever-unruly hair sliced in front like a chaperone.

"Show me your breasts?"

It was a question, not a command. I appreciated that. I lifted up my V-neck to reveal the frilly, embarrassingly juvenile training bra I had on underneath. I regretted the baby blue bow that graced the middle. All at once I felt like a kid again.

"You're gorgeous," he said, tugging my shirt down with controlled finality. Pride tugged at me. *Like that was enough. Like a glimpse could cure anything.*

My mother's frail voice pummeled me out of my mid-air thoughts:

"Maybe they didn't pull hard enough?" she offered. She looked surprised at her own vocalization.

"Stuck like glue," said the cop, rolling his feet — toe to heel. He smacked his lips and looked pointedly at my father. I wiggled my toes, which were dust-stained and in need of polish.

"How can she move like that?" My father gestured for a third time, happily jumping on my movement as a chance at another retort, "And not be taken down?"

"Sir, I was never much good at physics," replied the cop.

That night I was left to sleep dangling in the air like an out-of-sorts acrobat. After ushering the remaining stragglers away, promising explanations in the morning, my parents conversed in a few nods before waving me to "stay put," and went inside. My mother came out again and set up a cradle of bedclothes below on the trampoline, in case I should fall from my place in the night. My father reached up to give me the doll that I still childishly and determinedly slept with. She dangled, too, copying me.

My parents ate outside with me, sitting uncertainly on the trampoline like two kids on a first date, forks poised, hunger abated, hip bone to hip bone — a slightly askew picture of a family at dinnertime.

"Honey, you sure you're alright?" my mother asked, smoothing down my comforter for the fourth or fifth time.

"Yeah, Mom."

"I don't like leaving you out here like this," she said, expectant, as if I could come up with a solution for her worry.

"It's just the backyard," I said, as I stretched myself out horizontally, placing my doll on the soft part of my belly.

My mother looked at me with eyes that crinkled at the ends like Chinese fans. I realized that she'd be beautiful if only she shooed her constant anxiety away. I wondered if I was the cause of this.

"I'm fine," I reassured, as if to a child. "I'll see you in the morning."

I wasn't very bothered by this new turn of events. I'd never been that exceptional at anything. Adequate. Completely acceptable. Run-of-the-mill. These were the words that I, and others, used to describe me. I had the sort of features that were unremarkable to passersby. Unexceptionally pretty, all-American, with the obligatory stardust of freckles on a cherub nose, light gray eyes with light lashes, and an ordinary, undeveloped figure.

The stars winked at me from where I lay or levitated. I began to play a game I'd made up at my first sleepover years ago, to impress the group of girls that I'd gained admission to. I'd randomly select a number in my head and challenge myself to form a shape with that number of stars. If seven didn't work, I'd switch to ten, or thirteen, until I found a shape to satisfy my numbers. It smoothed over everything that was odd and angular in the world, into a system of patterns and wholeness.

Tonight, I counted to twenty-seven and made a pirate ship. I was missing one star in order to finish the final tip of the last sail, but I fell asleep in my breezed hammock before I could finish.

I awoke facing downwards, my blanket and doll having slipped and fallen during the night. She lay distorted on the trampoline, one cloth leg hanging off, facedown, her yellow curls wet with morning. Flipping over, I sat up to do away with the remains of a dream I couldn't quite remember.

"You're awake, then," said a voice from the play set.

I started, spinning like a top in the air to see Jimmy Timbers grinning at me from my old, abandoned childhood slide. He lounged on its long, red tongue, stretching out his well-formed calves that had always reminded me of grapefruit, digging the heels of his sneakers in the dirt.

"You're here," I said stupidly.

"Yep. My mom told me all about it, and I wouldn't miss this for the world!"

He grinned at me, and flipped his hair in one honeyed swoosh of bang.

"Yeah, weird, huh? Mom and Dad are pretty freaked."

I didn't know what to do with my hands or legs, so I clammed myself up in a ball, resting my knees into my chest, and moving a nervous hand through my tangled hair.

"I bet you're gonna be famous."

"Nah. I'm sure it's just a phase," I said, shrugging, equal parts delighted and embarrassed by his attention.

I could make out his moist upper lip where downy tufts of hair were beginning to grow like Easter grass. He was tanned and lean. His nose came to a perfect point — like an acute triangle.

"You should start charging admission or something," he said, as if this was the most brilliant idea ever thought up.

Jimmy was cute, and decidedly the most masculine fourteen-year-old in the neighborhood who, I had assured myself, also used tongue when he kissed; but even he could sometimes say something silly.

"I think my parents are looking for a specialist. Maybe I have some incurable disease."

The sudden thought of my toothy picture, bangs askew, my long bob tussled a little for effect — in a scientific thesaurus along with bolded caption and number like: **Figure 14.2. Amazing floating girl with special levitation abilities; thirteen-and-a-half; extraordinarily interesting and witty for her age.** It distracted me from Jimmy for a moment.

"You think I could get up there?" he asked.

I shook away my daydreams and realized with a vague pleasure that he looked wistful. I had something he wanted.

"I don't know. But let's try."

Beckoning him over, I told him to climb onto the trampoline until his head hit just below my knee. I felt his breath tickle my shin, and a shiver stirred up the nerves in my lower back like honeybees.

"On the count of three."

One, two, three, huff.

I pulled as he sprung up and began to climb into the air. His hand grasped my small forearm, and his face was so close to mine that I smelled peanut butter and contraband Pall Mall on his breath. I lunged forward — placing my face unnecessarily close. Then, he was gone, falling back with a bounce; he scowled up at me, and jumped to his feet again. My arms shook from his weight and our combined disappointment.

"Worth a shot," I said. I hoped he wasn't angry at me or ready to leave.

"It's alright. I guess it just means you're special."

He grinned a charming, lopsided smile that showed the edge of one of his canines.

"You look ferocious," I said, hoping I was a good enough flirt to keep him around a little longer.

Jimmy left with a promise to return and bring "more of the gang." As I watched him walk away from me, he lit a cigarette and tousled his hair once again. I wished I could follow.

Instead, I decided to test out just how resilient my new aerial placement actually was. I could stretch both sets of limbs out as far as they would go, but I couldn't move up or down. Even sideways was limited to two or three feet in each direction. It was as if I was in a strange box that could both withhold and expand, according to how liberal my movements were.

My father came out at some point, and stood watching me for a while with a grim look on his face. He held his coffee right under his chin, and I could see his glasses were fogging up. I made a mental note to invent glasses wipers — like windshield wipers but smaller and faster.

"Until we figure out what's up — eh — why you're stuck there, we're going to hire a little protection for you. Your mother doesn't want you out here in the open all of the time. Besides, the weather."

He looked up into the sky that was already graying into great tufts of clouds. I had to admit that he was right.

After consulting various policemen and hardware stores, the group of men that had now become a posse of sorts around me — the fat cop, a long-limbed fireman, my father — decided that renting a small-sized circus tent was the most practical solution.

"We'll get some guys out here, too," said the policeman, full of self-important pomp. I imagined him telling his wife how instead of rescuing a cat caught in a tree that he was in the process of rescuing a little girl from the air.

"I just don't like the idea of her out here," my mother repeated.

"Ma'am, we'll get some good, solid boys to look after your little girl," said the cop reassuringly. He smiled at my mother, and then looked back at my father, winking, as if to say *women, such frightened little things.*

It was an all-day ordeal, constructing my cage. The tent arrived in pieces: the nylon, cherry-red fabric that hurt my eyes, the solid, steel poles, and finally, my guards. There were two of them. One was an elderly gentleman, who looked more like a mall security cop than a crime-fighting, girl-protecting ninja. The other was Mr. Dempsy, to my surprise and delight. I'd forgotten that he worked as a security guard for various law offices in town. They looked up at me, and I down at them. We silently greeted one another as captor and captive for an intermittent period of time.

The tent was erected with the help of the policemen, my father, and my newly appointed guards. The tip swooped up in a straight V, five feet above my head. I felt claustrophobic in the thing, and begged for them to leave the door curtain open as wide as possible.

Inside, my mother laid out my belongings. She remade the pillow fort below, so if I fell, I'd be caught as softly as possible. A wheeled rack of clothes stood to my left, and the inflatable pool that I'd used as a child was to my right.

"For baths," my mother said in passing.

That night, I was restless, and eventually I called to Mr. Dempsy, who had been appointed as my night guard. He came inside quickly, asking me what was wrong.

"Can't sleep."

"You'll need your energy for tomorrow. Word's gotten out. You'll need your rest, little one, to take on the world tomorrow."

"You mean I'm famous?"

"You're the most exciting thing that's happened to this town in... well, since I can remember."

I grinned, and felt pleased that he thought so. I didn't want to be alone, then, so I asked him to sit right inside of the tent to keep guard.

"It gets lonely up here," I said coaxingly, hoping he'd relent and stay.

"As long as you promise to sleep like a good girl."

"I will."

Rolling over to face the back of the tent, I curled my body into a warm ball and listened to the katydids chirp their nightfall jubilee. I was asleep, soon, and unaware of the round, pale eyes that watched me in greedy takes from the tent's entrance.

I awoke to the sound of a bottomless voice that rang through my tent. I could hear, faintly, the protests of an older voice yelling that no one was allowed to be in here. *Here.* But where was here?

"Well hello there, Miss!" said the voice again, closer and louder than before.

A man of medium height, standard width, wearing the polyester suit of a mediocre bachelor strolled towards me. His shoes gleamed in the morning rays like two black toadstools.

I scrunched my nose up at him, tucking a strand of hair behind my ear that was rubbing against my flushed cheek.

"Hi," I said, sitting upright and crossing my legs. I brushed the sleep from my eyes as best I could, combing through my hair with stubby fingers. I could see the old security guard hobbling towards us in a fit of rage.

"You're like the Princess and the Pea in this get-up."

He whistled to himself as he looked around the tent. The eagerness of journalistic intrigue sparked his eyes. I didn't like him.

"You've never done this before?" I gestured to my neatly folded legs. A snarl curled my lower lip.

"Ha ha, you're a charmer, too, eh?" he said, shuffling his papers, and running a hand through his taupe hair.

"The crew's coming round. Say, where's your parents at anyway, doll?"

"I suspect they're inside."

"Don't go anywhere — ha," he said, appreciating his own joke and turning on his heel to make a beeline towards the back patio door. He passed the guard on his way out, clapping a quick hand on his knobby shoulder.

"Tried, ma'am. The bastard's a quick one," the old man said.

The reporter was back in five minutes with my parents in tow, talking over his shoulder as he strode purposefully back to me.

"You couldn't possibly think that this was going to stay a secret, now did you?" he asked.

"We were planning on it," my mother offered.

"Well that's just silly, little lady. Say, this your little sister hanging up there?"

Deeply crimson, my mother turned to burrow her cheeks into my father's lapel.

"What, exactly, are you planning on doing with my daughter?" asked my father. His hair was standing up at the ends, and his glasses were jammed into the pocket of his shirt, so he squinted ferociously in the direction of the reporter.

"Why, film, of course! This is breaking news. More news than this town has seen in ages."

He gestured towards his two cameramen, whose equipment was already angled towards me like machine guns. I cringed, and spun around so that all they could see was my back and the slight curve of my cheek.

"The public is gonna eat this up."

"We'd prefer privacy," said my father, glaring at the old guard and fishing in his pocket for his cell phone or gun – I wasn't exactly sure.

"Privacy, sir, is not going to happen. This is big, big, BIG! Besides, all we want for now is an interview. Think of it – we get this story out there and maybe, somewhere in this wonderful world of ours, some brilliant doctor will know what to do!"

He was good; I gave him that. He'd pushed the correct button: the "saving your daughter solution" that would persuade any parent. Soon enough, he had my father by the shoulder, leaning in, explaining what they would do, how they would film, and what stations my story would appear on.

I had to fight back my excitement that was spurred by his words. I couldn't help it. It had to come out.

"Let him film me," I said, rushing my words out before I could unsay them. My parents stared. "Maybe someone can help me."

"Well, there's going to be rules," my father said. He looked uneasy, glancing down at my mother's creased forehead.

"My daughter isn't going to become some freak show or something. Everyone must leave at nighttime. We have guards," he warned, shaking his finger at the reporter's paisley tie.

It happened fast: I was filmed, interviewed, and within the week, ropes sectioned me off from the rest of the world. People lined up in the streets, news anchors blocked driveways; neighbors, friends of neighbors, and people who'd seen me on television came to look at me, wave at me, call out questions about subjects ranging from the Second Coming to astrophysics. My parents, unsure, stood to the side and looked up at me. I said I was fine, that this is what needed to happen. And I enjoyed the attention, the looks of wonder that made me feel as if I'd done something big for once. I was glorious, a novelty, despite not having showered in two weeks. The pool had been punctured by a camera leg two days in.

At night, my father, shotgun in hand, iced-vodka in the other, waved away the onlookers and warned Dempsy that if someone so much as set foot on his lawn, he'd shoot them.

The night before an especially big TV interview, my mother attempted to sponge me off. The interview would premiere on one of those shiny news channels that my father used to shake his fist at, when he had time for television. I was in dire need of a little polishing. My nerves sang in my ears as I thought about what dress I should wear.

My mother scuttled up onto the trampoline, handed me one soaped up sponge in sweet-smelling jasmine, drenching my white, unshaven legs with the other, in the moonlight. We avoided each other's eyes, but the feel of her hand on my shins made me shiver with want. I missed being touched.

I wrung the sponge into my hair and was surprised by the feel of dampness besides my own sweat and dew. She pulled shaving cream from her robe pocket and began to lather my legs in the foamy stuff. I closed my eyes and felt the soft nudge of the razor scraping away.

We didn't talk; I really hadn't talked to anyone since I'd decided on my fame. I was beginning to feel more and more detached from this place. Everything seemed three times as beautiful and twice as clear. I was caught, juxtaposed against the harsh reality of where I was, and the aching sensation that I had the ability to transcend it all if I only knew how. And in my mind, it was fame. To push myself until I burned out and dropped once more onto my trampoline, cocooned in gravity. I was growing tired of suspension, but I was terrified of losing it.

The interview was early the next morning. A storm had rolled through overnight. I was still shaken by the memory of the tent's roiling shape and the sound of dark rain so close to my head. My mother had given me a red ribbon to tie my hair back with — it had begun growing much faster in my elevated state, and was now to my shoulders. The reporter asked if I liked all of this, and for a moment I was unsure of what to say. I wanted to scream at him and rip my bow and wave it in surrender. Instead I said yes, yes I did. I hid my trembling hands in the folds of my navy dress.

"And how do you think you got up there, anyways, Miss?"

"I think it was an accident."

"In what way, an accident?"

"The Earth's fault."

I'd thought the reason over for many nights. It must have been something in the air when I took that fateful jump.

The world, somehow, forgot itself, or slipped to the side and everything was skewed. And it was timing, and it was that deep wish of mine I'd carried around for so long — for something exciting to happen to me. Maybe the Earth heard that finally, and forgot the rules for a moment.

"I think I got stuck like a star does, when it's born. But I'm not some piece of space; I'm human."

I heard the question in my voice before the sentence was finished. I'm human. A girl. I'm not a bit of rock and dust that has no choice but to stand up in the sky. I realized my hands were outstretched in a see? *This is what I am, see? This is flesh and a pile of bones that contains life!*

"A... star?"

"Yes, and when they fall, they crash to the Earth again and their light goes out."

"And do you think you will crash?"

"Most definitely. Any day now," I said, as I untied my bow and let it fall to the ground. There's always an ending. I looked into the reporter's face.

After the interview, Jimmy stayed behind. He had on a backwards baseball cap so that his long hair peeped out in pale tufts. He was the most beautiful boy I'd ever seen, and for some reason, this made me angry.

"I wanted to ask you something," he said.

"What's that?"

"Will you be my girlfriend?"

"Why now?" I said, suddenly suspicious. "Why not before when I could walk with you, and go to the movies with you?"

"Because... I don't know. Why does it matter? I'm asking now."

"I think it's too late."

"No. It's not."

He looked petulant. I realized that we were two children playing at love. A slippery love.

"I'm stuck here, Jimmy. Didn't you even listen? I can't even hold hands with you."

"It doesn't matter," he said.

"Oh, but it does. It matters so much," I said. "I've got everything I need."

I saw the hurt in his eyes, and it made me glad.

That night as I lay looking into the tent folds, I heard soft steps on the grass that my father had now let go to seed. Thinking it was Jimmy again, I remained silent, feigning sleep.

"I know you're awake, little one," said Mr. Dempsy.

I rolled over to see him standing in the tent's entrance, outlined by the black night. He let his flashlight dangle at his side.

"I overheard your conversation from earlier," he said. "Jimmy's a silly boy. Don't you let boys like that go breaking your heart."

"I'll try not to," I said, smiling. I knew it was a sad smile. It felt sad. The corners of my mouth had turned hard, and it felt stuck there.

"Can I come up?"

Heaving his wiry body onto the trampoline, he stood, the top of his head reaching the top of my sternum.

"So how do you do this?" he asked, like he was puzzling over a new hobby.

"I'm not sure. I just... jumped, and here I am now."

"Well let's give it a try."

He began to bob up and down, unsteady and tentative, but then gained momentum. His bounces became surer of themselves, his face a metamorphosis of trepidation, fear, glee, then, determination — and he sprang up, his tie flipping against gravity and tapping against his nose. He didn't catch; he wasn't stuck like me. And he fell back again, panting, boyish, his limbs spread eagle-style. His white button-down shirt had come undone at the bottom. The intimate skin of his belly shone, exposed in the night's shadows.

"Damn, that's fun," he said, hoisting himself up again and tugging his shirt down.

"I know," I said, biting back a sob. "Shouldn't you be watching to see if... if anyone comes?"

"In a minute. It's late, and you look upset."

I felt sick to my stomach. The excruciating privacy of a shirt undone, a portion of body exposed, a man so sad and quiet to the world that he jumps on children's play things like an overgrown, awkward boy. It was all these things, and the feeling it gave me, of looking on at a tragedy.

"What's wrong?"

"Nothing," I lied, refusing to meet his puffy eyes and realize just how much of a fool I was. I represented the raw form of his housewives. Again, I was a novelty.

I felt my face being touched by his dry fingers. They felt like petals. The heated points traced miniature columns down my cheeks, routing the course of my tears. He was fully standing again and leaned in towards me, for once, sure of himself. I kept still and oblivious. His lips searched for mine, but he was clumsy and unpracticed, and he missed, pressing his stubble into the right side of my cheek, below my lip; I shook in my bones.

He began to grope — there were fast snatches of skin and slight and unintentional tugs of hair. Where he touched, goosebumps raised themselves up like mushrooms. A chemical reaction. He touched and learned me right down to my very knees. They say in books it's as if a man's touch memorizes you. This was not memorization, but simply rote memory, an artificial, physical learning that kept pace with his movements — learning enough to fulfill a desire that would be met, would not stand not to be met.

I felt at once desired and repulsive, an object on display like my mother's prized wedding china, groveled at and scraped clean. His breath was sour with tart beer — I realized he was drunk. My body had become expendable. He slipped my navy shorts down, fumbling with the small zipper with impassioned fingers, and as he did, I, myself, lowered a little. At first I thought I was imagining it, but he now rose over me. I was unreachable no longer.

I felt a dull thud in me, like a drum mixed up in its own rhythm. He grabbed my waist and pressed me into him so that my face met his chest. I got a mouthful of dried sweat and more of the awful beer. He pulled me into a measured tempo of forwards and back, swaying in the air, rocked by a man deep within himself. I tasted blood, and realized I'd been biting my tongue.

I kept on lowering. And because of it, I couldn't scream. I only had the constant, aching memory of suspension among my backyard's eucalyptus trees. I couldn't alert the universe to this monumental mistake. He pushed and heaved, grabbing my forearms tighter, rough; I wasn't me, it wasn't me, I am not me, I am not, I am.

I finally lay on the trampoline, grateful that he'd cried out in pain — I hoped it was pain — sweat gathered on my brow in puddles of salt. He knelt above me, his spindle legs splayed on either side of me. He gasped for breath in the warm night, and I lay still, feeling the trickle and thrum inside me like a harp. I felt like an inside-out sock. So this was it.

He left after that. Realizing what he'd done, he fastened his pants and laid a wet palm on my shoulder in a gesture of what? Sorrow? A mute "thanks"? A reconciliatory pat to stop me from telling? He looked gaunt and hollowed out. I hoped that's what I'd done to him — damaged him too, right into the very core of middle-aged sadness. His glance was meaningful, but I didn't allow myself to understand the message.

I lay there still, lowering my hand to where he'd knocked and knocked and knocked until the atmosphere grew tired and renounced me, shackling me to the ground like the small, foolish mortal I was; it was slick with pink.

SHE

HAPHAZARD ANGLES *and the lovely curve of shoulder bone, he recognizes these small intricacies like constellations, as intimate as his heartstrings.*

She reaches for a coffee and tucks her wallet back into her pocket, all the while jiggling her left foot, full of impatience. He stands outside of the shop, watching her through the thin glass like he always does when he sees her, a few steps away for good measure, uncertainty claiming him. Her hair is shiny like wood finish, the curls individually separated and falling halfway down her back in a perfect river tangle. It isn't tied up anymore like it had been at the funeral. He wonders where that ribbon has gone – it had been burgundy and velvet and perfect.

This is the third time he's seen her in a month. She's a focal point in an inane, senseless day. He never catches her face. It's merely the rounded tip of a cheek, the tiny tug at the corner of her mouth, a dimple, and an eyelash. But the full on effect is just the same. It's her.

He always follows her when he sees her. He knows she'll end up disappearing, shaking him off her scent with a brutality that makes him long for her touch again. It's the stuff of dreams, chasing a dead woman. She cuts hearts on her teeth like clamshells.

• • •

They'd met in college on a cigarette break. She smoked, but only smoked others'. "You're not a smoker if you don't buy your own," she said. They were taking one of those English seminar classes that tried to cram every major literary work into the mix — Kafka, Yeats, Byron, Elliot, Austen, a smattering of Marquez to round out the globe more nicely.

"You read?" she asked.

"Skimmed," he said, eyeing her flatly; his lids ached from mid-morning hangover.

"These unfiltered?" She took another drag, turning it around in her fingers like a magician's coin.

He nodded, and shouldered away from her as a gust of cold February wind knocked against him.

"I can't believe we're reading *Catcher in the Rye* in a 400 level. I always hated that book. I read it when I was really young and I called my dad a phony because I thought it sounded nice. He grounded me for a week."

"So, no classics for you? What's your poison?" he asked.

"Oh, I'm fine with the classics. But I like dystopian, just like any other self-respecting cynic."

She smiled, then. There was lip-gloss stuck to her tooth, and that was when he realized she was beautiful. Her hair shone white against the mid-morning sun blaze, and there was a dark mole on the left side of her nostril that he'd thought was a nose ring for the past two months of class. Her face had flushed around the apples of her cheeks like two searing, red stars. Her eyes were an unimpressive brown, but they were wide, so wide, forest-wide.

• • •

He sees her in the company of others, never alone, as if she might cease to exist, like a collective idea. But that's exactly what she is — a collection of forgotten things, wishes, and the small cruelties of the day-to-day.

• • •

They went to party together at someone's girlfriend's house and she told him to pick up a bottle of Merlot before he picked her up that night. She'd fallen into the habit of reliance, but it was sternly dictated, demanded by her.

He raked the bottles of wine with his eyes and decided on one that looked elegant, was less than thirteen dollars, and had a beige band of vintage grapes running around its neck. He'd been in a strange flux of wanting to impress and repel the past couple of weeks.

The party was in a cramped house with bare walls. There was a cat that hid in the laundry room. It seized up when its owner drunkenly snatched it up, holding it over everyone's heads like Simba from *The Lion King*.

"This is the best goddamn cat in the world!"

People murmured, shifting themselves about. She didn't look pleased. As soon as the cat was let go, she followed it into a dark laundry room, sat cross-legged on the floor, and stroked its right ear with the crook of her finger.

He stood in the open doorway simultaneously watching her and the party. He chugged his beer and waved to her that he would get another. He felt uncomfortable when she wasn't near him.

31

She ignored his gesture, burying her face in the cat's scraggly fur. When he got back, she knocked the door closed with the tip of her sandal. Her face was slim and silver in the narrow light, and she grinned at him, her lipstick a chocolate smear. The cat stretched itself out in her lap, pawing at the air.

"So, you love me, right?" She didn't say this to his face, but to her ankles, hiding in her mane of hair.

"Yes, probably." He shrugged, bumping her arm with his, feeling electric.

• • •

He follows her out of the store and onto the bright street, and the wind bites at his face. A careful pause. She winds the scarf around her neck, brushing her hair out into that long stream, and walks. Before long, a corner takes her and she's gone as always. He circles around a few times, strumming distracted fingers in his pocket. He gives up and goes home to an empty apartment.

That night he makes lasagna like she likes it. He pours a glass of Merlot and sits at the kitchen table. The cat is asleep under the table, heaved onto its side like a lump of orange dust. He doesn't like Italian food, and wine makes him tired, but there's always a vague masochism to this process wrapped in a vague hope that she'll come home if he makes it just right.

• • •

Drugs weren't an issue until after graduation and they got serious and stopped going to parties. They moved in together, claiming that taking a few years off to live was a rite of passage for the newly anointed adult. She left hair in the bathroom, and in uncanny places that seemed to mark boundaries — the shower wall, commode lever, and wound around the faucet like a ribbon. She screamed at spiders, and he loved her for that.

Syringes began to appear on the coffee table, leaning in day-old coffee cups like space-age straws; blackened spoons, pink Bic lighters caught in the wayward mess of lint and pennies in her coat pockets. He tried it with her once; didn't like it much. He got these aching sunspots behind his eyes that made his brain feel like sheep's wool.

"You know, it's used to treat end-stage cancer. This is my own form of terminal," she'd say. He thought she was being funny and glib and charming. Then she'd heat up the spoon and forget about him and the cat. She was ritualistic with it, as if this was her art. She was beating to windward, leaving them far behind.

• • •

After her first appearance, about a year after her death, he'd done some research online about PTSD and other hallucinogenic phenomenon. "I see dead people," was his first Google search term; he realized the absurdity of the situation. Apparently, it wasn't uncommon to see loved ones who were deceased. The Internet's assurance of its commonality just made him angry. *Sensory perception without external stimulation of the relevant sensory organ* didn't mean anything to him, just some words used to explain away the impossible. She was here, and she wasn't. One time, he smelled her perfume. It had always been the same, a musky scent that reminded him of Sundays and twilight. If he was being haunted, she wasn't very good at it.

• • •

"You can't keep on doing this. You don't even play with the cat anymore," he said, when he came home from work and found her half-unconscious, the cat mewing at an empty food bowl, and the house smelling like tar. She had lost the last girlishness to her face. Now, it was narrow, boasting a chin too pointed for the rest of it, like a witch out of a fairy-tale.

But there wasn't any need for conversation now. She was rocked by something larger than him, and she was spread out, limp-limbed like a rag doll. She had lost her job two weeks before — an office assistant in an eye clinic with people she said she wished were dead or worse. He picked up the cat, taking it into the kitchen, and started running water. Dropping the cat onto the counter, he doused his head into the sink, willing himself to love her enough, to love her a little better than this.

Whoever it was who supplied her with the stuff gave her something so unalloyed and clean that she couldn't handle it. He had his suspicions; probably the crackhead couple on the first floor with their goofy smiles and unwashed bodies and crying jags he could hear from underneath the floorboards. Weepy things that stung at his nerves. But they had a kid and their kitchen smelled like baby powder. They ate jarred carrots and potato mush.

The purity and the can opener ultimately did it. And time — yes, time, the thing she had always wished she had more of. There were days when she refused to shower, foregoing a life she'd put on mute. There was dust that swirled in the air and pillows soaked in sweat from her many midday naps.

"Why are you unhappy?" he asked.

"I'm not unhappy. No, really, I'm not. Just trying to figure things out."

She would look at him with out-of-focus eyes, their color more dull and dark than he'd ever seen them before. He didn't recognize this thin-haired girl anymore, and he knew she didn't recognize him, either.

She had just slammed, and was opening a can of cat food in the kitchen before the full euphoria sent her into that glorious daze, when she swayed backwards and crashed into the kitchen chair. She hit her neck, a central point that curved her chin up to an impossible level. The can rolled into the hallway, the cat hissed. He knocked over his beer at the sound.

At the hospital, there were papers to sign and he met her parents for the first time. Her mother was tiny, sparrow-like, with over-large spectacles that framed red-rimmed calico eyes, which darted over him in vague distaste. Her father was bent, beer-bellied, and white-haired.

"I loved her, you know. I have her stuff at the house. We have a cat," he said. Her father gave him a dead-eyed look and shuffled the papers.

Later, when he finally got home, he slid down onto the cold tile of the kitchen, and *chck-chck-chcked* for the cat to come to him. It settled itself on his knees and looked up at him with an expectant, yellow glare.

"What now, Cat?"

• • •

A couple of weeks after seeing her in the coffee shop, he is on his lunch break at the job he's failed to quit. Little things seem so hard now — a two-week's notice, buying resealable cat food. He threw away the can opener.

She's there again, standing at a red light. Her back hunches as if she's carrying something. The ribbon is back — reclaiming her. Green, go; he follows her four blocks until she stops outside a housewares store with an OUT OF BUSINESS sign taped to the door. She turns to look into its window, and he catches a glimpse of her profile and of what she's carrying. It's a box filled with utensils — specifically, spoons of all sizes like bright, metal puzzle pieces. Some are rubber-capped like a baby's; others have gilded designs of carnations on their stems; there are colored handles in seashore colors: plastic, antique, and an absinthe spoon.

She kicks the door open with her foot, adjusting the box more carefully into the crooks of her arms so that her right shoulder angles against the street and sky, and she is gone.

LIGHT LANGUAGE

MY FAMILY IS IN THE FIREFLY BUSINESS. I like watching the bugs flit about in their fragile, glass containers. Their elongated, ochre bodies are tipped with ruby on the head with a delicate yellow globe of light on the bottom, suspended and hollow. It reminds me of miniature fires that are continuously snuffed out and rekindled, ruled by cosmos. They are so quick and delicate, furtive in their short life spans. Their wings are perfect, almost navy, save for a few inordinate shades of pearl.

I've named my favorites. The fat one, the male, I've named Hotaru. He is greedy with his nectar, and is constantly illuminated, aggressive and kingly. His wife — a real golden beauty — I've christened Lucciola. My mother tells me not to do this; she's afraid I'll get too attached. I name them anyway. I like the idea of bits of me spread out over the world.

Today, my mother sifts through a pile of bills. She pats me on the top of my head with her left hand, and strokes my rough rope of a braid. Her hands are lovely and sad. Father likes to recount how he fell in love with those hands. *At first sight. A straight arrow into my heart. My God, I worshipped them.*

"Go find your sister. She's supposed to help me with these," Mother says, nodding toward the neat stack and nibbling at her pen top. "And I know *you* won't do any good."

She is teasing me. It is gentle.

"John — the alchemist, I mean — is coming for tea to discuss some business. I'd like to get these paid and sent out by three," she stumbles to explain.

Bright patches of heat. A shy glance. These are the things I notice.

Recently, my mother has seemed more cheerful. She hums little tunes to herself in our bright kitchen. She is nervous, twisting her rings, all chatter, jittering about, her apron loosely tied in a wilting bow. Having made friends with the new alchemist, she regularly invites him over for tea or talk. He's shy, and blushes a good deal of the time. I think he feels more comfortable with his boiling glasses and funnels than he does with my beautiful mother and her two waifish daughters. I'm glad she has a friend, since Father is usually outside with his flies, dreaming, and the women in town are predisposed to more trivial activities than charting bug statistics.

I'm a twin. The less pretty one, but my father's undisputed favorite. We're the dreamers in the family. My mother and sister, Daphne, are on the business end of things here at the bungalow. The only way you can tell my sister and me apart, besides her prettiness, is our eyes. Mine turned out mossy and dark, *ancient and wise, like those wild things,* the midwife had told my exhausted mother fifteen years ago. My sister's maintained the warm, honey-brown color of my parents'. She's very good with her eyes. I've seen people melt into them, charmed by their size and hue. I find mine strange.

Father calls me Kitten, because he says they glow in the dark like a cat's.

I find my sister sitting at the kitchen table, scribbling numbers, her hair tied up in a messy bump. We are both pale and freckled; while mine are a constant cause of concern and embarrassment, she wears hers well.

"Daphne, Mama wants to see you."

"Tell her I'm finishing up some calculations. We've gone way over budget this month. Gonna have to cut back on a few things."

"Like what?"

"For starters, we need to reduce all the nectar we're importing. Those gypsies down at the bayou that sell it give me the creeps. Do you even know how expensive that stuff is?"

At this, she looks up at me for the first time. Incredibly lovely as always. Bright eyes and all frenetic with purpose.

"No."

"Of course you don't. You and Father just like planning ways to spend money."

"We've got to feed them," I say, defensive.

"The Milkweed nectar we've been using is exorbitant! We have a business to run. As long as we keep those bugs alive, I'd say we're doing pretty well."

"The Milkweed makes their lights stronger. Father and I proved that to you and Mother last month."

"It's a light. As long as they're lit, and buzzing, we're good. I was happy with the nectar from the Turk's Cap."

"It smelled funny," I say.

"You smell funny," she retorts, back to her papers, a dismissal.

Arguments with my sister never end well. She gets red-faced and threatens to go back to school and leave our farm to rot. But I know she never will. The people at school were far crueler to Daphne than she lets on. One time, about three years ago, she came home with a crescent-mooned gash on the tip of her cheek. It was swollen for days, and then turned purple like the jellyfish we caught one summer back when we were children, when Father took us to the seashore. She never once cried, but I recognized the hurt in her eyes just the same.

"Go find Mother when you're done, Hothead," I say in mid-turn through the doorway.

I walk into the slate-gray shed to visit the fireflies. We've separated the males and females for mating purposes. The males are my favorite, in part because they're the hardest workers. Father says they use their fire more because it's their way of blinking love to the ladies. He always chuckles to himself at this. Sometimes, Father and I will turn off the lights and sit on the straw ground, watching the tiny fireworks show. To me, it's like watching them burst out into the darkness: a sacred, small thing.

I place my forefinger on the nearest of the glass jars. This draws a stray fly up to it like a Plasma globe. Its wings are almost imperceptible through the thick glass. It quivers and then zips away to the other side of the jar, turning somersaults in the air — a lightning bug circus of sorts.

"Hello, Sweetheart."

I hear soft padding behind me on the earth floor, and turn to find my father standing in the doorway. He grins at me. I run towards him and clasp my arms around his steady chest.

"Visiting our friends?"

"I just came from Daphne. Milkweed is too expensive."

"Humbug! Expenses. Let's just worry over these little guys," he says, nodding to the closest jar of flies.

"Can we take the bugs out tonight, Father?"

"Of course, it's a full moon."

And he gives me that wild, adoring look — wide-eyed and mouth splayed open in a sloppy grin that is truly, wonderfully terrifying.

It is after dinner, and the deep, velvet glow of the day is just barely peeking over the treetops. The weather is still balmy, but there is a damp chill in the shadows, and the grass is wet with dark. I look back towards our home — dim and compact against the backdrop of Grancy Gray-Beards and Loblolly Pines. We are adjacent to the Mermentau River, a few miles north of Skull Island.

My father holds the metal lantern in his right hand, and a case of four glass jars filled with fireflies in his left. I walk behind his soft steps, carrying six more of the jars, meticulously balancing them in every possible crook of my body. When we reach our usual place by the river's edge, we set the jars down. I scan the lemon-green land bordering it. I always look for bones that may have washed up from the island. I found a finger bone once, or so Father says. I was quite young, and had escaped the family picnic to explore the river's grim underbrush. I'd come running back, my little cheeks stinging with excitement, flourishing a grey-brown stick. It turned out to be part of a finger. Mother, of course, was horrified; Daphne began to cry. Father had picked it from my small fingers and laid it out onto his palm. We later washed it off several times, scraping away the time-grown grime. We set it out to float down the river again, a friendly offering to the swamp spirits.

"You ready?" he asks, unscrewing the top to a jar. Instead of answering, I grab a jar for myself, twist the top off, and watch as a cloud of bright bugs explode into the night air. I hear the familiar buzz, one bumps into my cheek, and I feel the soft tickle of wings. It smells sweet here.

"They're so happy," I say, exposing my neck to the stars.

My father and I have been taking our bugs out for a fly for years now. We experienced a few dozen deaths from keeping them cooped up, so Father remedied this by arranging nightly strolls. We've trained them to come back to us. Even the smallest of creatures recognizes kindness.

We sit there for an hour, letting the flies play. They spin, light on our fingertips, teasing us. Sometimes we hear the swamp spirits' calls. It's a lonely sound, but not frightening. All I feel for them is pity. They belong to the weeds, making their dwellings near Skull Island, bound by an eternal mourning.

My father places two fingers to his mouth and lets out a clear whistle when it is time to go. We gather our bugs, now demure, sleepy and sedate with exercise. I look around once more to the shaded river and see nothing.

It is morning, and my jasmine duvet cover is bathed in fresh sunshine. The smell of Colombian coffee has infused our room. I get out of bed, placing my feet on the scraped oak floor. The crumbs from my late-night sauerkraut sandwich stick to the bottoms of my toes like snow. I walk down the wooden steps to the kitchen and hear Daphne's raspy morning voice.

"Honestly, Mother, it's not like they'll even notice. They're bugs."

"I know. It's just what Papa and your sister will say. You know how attached they get. And I don't think your father likes the new alchemist that much. His predecessor was a friend of his. "

"Some friend. Leaving that suicide note tacked to the shed out there. Creepy."

"Still, there's bad blood there. You know your father."

"Mother, this is a business," Daphne says, her voice thick with impatience. "And it's just a sedative. It's not like we're killing them. And even if the first batch doesn't work out, we'll know what to adjust for the other ones."

I finish walking down the steps, and see my sister's face contort, nostrils flaring. My mother looks nervous and ceases to spoon sugar into her mug.

"What sedatives?"

"It's just—" my mother begins. Daphne cuts her short.

"Oh, God, Kitten. It's just a way of cutting costs for food. We'll be able to easily transport them, too."

"Sweetheart, it's just a way to get them to cooperate a bit better. It's easy for the customers. They wake up after, anyways. We've been talking to the new alchemist in town. He's given us a good bargain. And, we're just using a small batch to experiment on. So if anything does go wrong...."

Mother glances at Daphne for reassurance.

"We? I've never seen her talking to him," I say, directing my glare at my sister.

The alchemist stayed late last night. He and mother drank endless cups of tea from her wedding china. She and Father haven't used them in forever. And his eyes were hot and her skin looked milky in the lamplight.

"But what if it doesn't work? What if they die? Does Father even know about this?"

"We were going to tell him soon," my sister says.

"Soon? This is his business. Those are his bugs."

45

"Father's a dreamer and an irresponsible business man."

"Last time I checked, we were pretty well off. Also, who made you in charge?"

Daphne squints her almond eyes at me. Her delicate features are pinched and flushed. I run out the door, flinging myself into bright sunshine.

My father — ritualistic and steady as always — is feeding nectar into the jars with a large syringe. He looks up when he hears the soft crunch of gravel from my bedroom slippers.

"Kitten, what's up? We just got new larvae in. Wanna look? They're beauts!"

"Do you know about the formula or whatever they're planning on feeding our flies? The alchemist. Some experimental sleep."

He looks at me blankly. The syringe hovers over the jar, a tiny amount of yellow nectar caught in its tip.

"The alchemist?" he says.

"Mother said he's been talking with her about some sort of sleep medicine for the bugs."

"Finish the feeding."

He stands abruptly, dusting off invisible specks of dirt, and leaves me alone with the bugs' breakfast.

I'm taking the bugs out alone tonight. The air feels dusty. My mind is a rapid-fire succession of questions. I have never seen my parents fight outright. Their marriage is in a constant state of flux, but it's a silent thing that no one discusses. The flies are lazy tonight. They glide — almost hover — in the breeze like dandelion seeds. I watch them, twisting my fingers back and forth until they are red and ache. My father once said that his greatest fear was to sell his bugs into the wrong hands. To enforce twilight on these things seems like a murder, because they choose their owners. It's something my father prides himself on — the unique relationship that he allows to form between customer and fly.

A fly nudges me on the tip of my nose, surprising me into the dusk again. It zips away, blinking. I pluck at a few strands of Bermuda grass, and toss them towards the water. I watch a cottonmouth raise itself from the river — a languid, silent "S" figure.

We are a disappearing people. This land of ours is a precious thing. The water claims us each and every year. The few families we know are diminishing, and sometimes I wonder whether they are also swallowed up by the sea along with their lands. The bottomland hardwoods that nestle our home are so silent these days. I cut my wrist on a Cypress knee once. They look like the earth's daggers with their sharp, nettled points.

The shed is lit at once with the collective blaze from the jars. The flies that I'd left behind — the ones from last night, as well as the new larvae — greet us with glow. Their familiar light language makes me waver on my decision, because what is goodness when everything's in shadow?

"I'm about to do something terrible," I confess to them. "But I think it's less terrible than what could happen to you."

I pause, lulled by the sound, the warmth — this fabricated safety that I have come to know so well. I rub salt from my eyes, and smell the swamp in my hair. One by one, I open them: the dozens of copper and brass lids that hold our entire livelihood, letting the thick glass fall to the straw floor. I sense the bugs' confusion at this unceremonious gesture. They fly out, pausing, swaying, some dipping towards the nectar hoses that are neatly looped on the wall like lassos. I hear footsteps approaching.

"What on earth are you doing?" Daphne says, a ghost of a girl against the night.

"Go," I say, ushering, waving the continuous tide away from me.

She steps forward, grappling for the jar I hold in my hand. When I avoid her, she grasps at the bugs themselves. Her hand closes around one, and I hear a sickly smoosh from her fist.

"You killed it!" I scream. I lunge towards her, pry her hand open, and see something terrible and brown in the middle of her glowing palm. It's smeared with firefly fluid and I feel sick. I slap her across the cheek. I turn, then, and run towards the remaining bugs, waving my arms in mad shooing motions. Sensing danger, the flies begin releasing their blood juice. It stings my face as the small, acid droplets fall like a night shower. Daphne stands watching me, wiping her smeared hand against her nightgown.

"Go, just go, please," I beg. "I'm throwing you out!"

Once they are gone, I fall to my knees, retching as a rush of nausea overtakes me. My face throbs with the flies' poison, and I smear the cold mud on my cheeks like war paint. Letting out a loud sob, I curl into a ball. I feel my sister standing over me.

"You know, you just ruined everything," she says, her voice steel. "You're so stupid."

"It wasn't right," I say.

"Right? You and Father are so caught in the ethics of this imaginary world you've dreamed up. Have you ever stopped and considered that it — this — isn't real? I'm going to bed. This is your mess. Clean it up."

I wake on the floor of the shed, stiff with sleep and incredibly dirty. I shift, rising, gingerly avoiding the particular stiffness in my neck. Raising my head to the door, I see my Father sitting on the oak bench, watching me.

"Father."

"I know why you did it."

I don't know how to respond, so I continue sitting up. I draw my dirtied knees to my chin and cradle it between them.

"What you did was wrong," he says, "but I understand."

He offers a tight smile, but there is no gladness around his lips. He looks at me, and at once I see heaviness in his eyes.

"Your mother left this morning. She's... she's staying in town for now. With Daphne." He looks humbled. The steadiness is all gone.

"We are alone."

"The alchemist?"

"Yes."

There's an emptiness to these words. There's a finality to them that refuses hope or any clear ending in sight.

"What about the larvae?" I ask, finally, distracted by the thought of my twin's absence.

"We still have that."

He shifts, running a hand through his thinning hair. This man is no longer my father.

No one attends the fly's funeral besides me. It's a windy day. The clouds hang in low ripples in the sky, and the earth is beginning to think like summer. I found a cardboard box that used to contain a pair of earrings I'd been given for a birthday years ago. I've nestled a small Christmas light on some cotton inside of the box. With a few large sticks, I've poked and plodded a hole in the earth. It is shallow but the best that I can do. I place the box into the hole, fitting it in — a small square in an awkward circle. Rising up, I cover the hole with my foot. I stamp down on it, flattening the earth, giving it my own imprint, or blessing.

Legba

I WAS AT THE CROSSROADS, and a man was there.

His smallness was exacerbated by the wide-brimmed straw hat that was crooked low over his face. At first, I thought it was black, but the sun beat down and I shielded my eyes and at once it was red. A deep ruby. So deep that it turned black once more. He clutched at his cane — a sleek mahogany — the only thing that wasn't legends old about him. His hat tipped so that I could only make out one cheek and one eye — a startling, oppressive white that looked well and weird between the crinkles on his face. Spider hands. A deeply hunched back that still held a surplus of dignity. He gave a grin to no one in particular, teeth flashing a mangy yellow, parted neatly in the middle by two gold incisors. His eye was so milky that the pupil looked distorted — too small for the eye's oblong shape, losing itself in color like a rowboat at sea.

"Daughter," he said.

I mopped a wisp of red hair out of my face, and locked my knees together in a strange impulse of respect for this old-timer. My hair had turned feral, wild like the azalea bushes at home, and still smelled like the hospital, taken to sticking itself across my left eyebrow like a head wound. I stood there, conscious of my dusty, hospital dress, my hair — tress by tress — in dizzying motion, and the sweat that tugged at my face like a mask.

"A long journey, it seems."

It was neither a question nor a statement, but regardless, a reply hung there. My mouth was dry, rusted shut. I stared, hating myself for seeming foolish, mute, in front of this man who I knew, without question, could provide answers.

He hobbled towards me. His right leg stuck out at a duck foot's angle, reminding me of a hockey stick. But he was agile, still, directing his cane straight into the softest spots of dappled Mississippi mud. He aimed without looking, his salient eye fixed on me, and I stood there waiting. And his hat — oh, that damnable, beautiful hat. It changed again with each reflection of Southern sun.

"Was it long?"

"So long," I said. "And still not finished."

I exhaled in tangible relief. Words, it seemed, were a commodity after all.

"Do you want it to be?" he asked.

"I don't know. Something is wrong with it."

"So, will you leave now? Sacrifice its life for your death?"

I couldn't find words for a response and shrugged. His one eye appraised me. I saw the pupil dilate a millimeter, and felt embarrassed.

"My job is not to judge. My job is to ensure a passage," he said.

"A successful one, I hope?" I tried a sly smile, a bartering of false suggestions — cuteness — the thing I put to practice with old men and strangers.

"That isn't up to me, Daughter."

"But, they said its neck was possibly broken. And there were other things. Abnormalities. Isn't it kind to let that type of thing pass from the world without pain?"

"Is it the thing's pain that you are concerned about?"

He turned and shuffled back towards the crossroads, abruptly finished with me. I was surprised, expecting a righteous speech, a thrusting in the correct direction that absolved me from any choice of my own.

"Hey! Where're you going?"

"I'd suggest you decide. Your husband is tired."

I watched him hobble back to his corner of the roads. It took far longer than it had for him to reach me. But finally, he was there, stooped, again, to a child's height. He breathed in, and sank lower into himself and was still — a grey scarecrow.

"Fucking psychopomp," I said, irritated and disappointed. Tears and dust muddled my vision. I stepped backwards, eyes screwed up against the elements and emotion. A red noise rang in my ears.

I was back in the hospital room, away from the mud and heat. My legs, twisted in bedclothes, were swollen and a thick sheet of perspiration sealed hospital gown to skin. Daniel was standing on my left side, twisting my sticky fingers into little knots, and then stroking them out, flattening them against his large, brown palm.

"Hello," I said.

"You passed out on us again, Lorelai."

"I know."

"The doctor just left to see about options. A C-section isn't possible because she's somehow wedged herself nearer your spine."

"She?"

My mind was a step slower than usual, and forming words took a decent amount of trouble.

"Our daughter."

"Daniel, this — thing. It's not our daughter."

"What do you mean?"

"Didn't you hear him?"

"Baby, you're exhausted. And that medicine. Jesus — they really pump it into you."

"You really think we could be happy raising something like this?" I asked, ignoring his soothing tone.

He started to say something, but my vision took on a marbled hue of green and amber. There was the nurse, and that pleasant humming of needle in vein. Her hands, brumal on my skin, were quick in their movements. Daniel's lips moved, smiling down at me, rubbing my shoulder through the thin material.

Like he could possibly understand anything.

This began the night that Father died. Daniel and I had been upstairs asleep in my childhood bed with the dowdy, chintz wall draping that my father's second ex-wife had claimed was charming. After she'd realized that an old Southern name didn't always mean a trust fund, she took off, but not before arranging orders of ornate and vaguely phallic accouterments to decorate our large, decidedly dilapidated old home.

The wind had picked up — it had been the kind of sleepy hot earlier in the day that nestled itself in the corners of rooms like a lazy, sun-fed cat, eliciting yawns from even the sharp-eyed day nurse. I'd kept the window halfway open because my room, adjacent to the attic, had the habit of heating up to over eighty degrees.

Slipping on a pair of wool socks in case of splinters, I descended the stairwell, gingerly avoiding the worn-in step that let out a drunkard's shout when stepped on. It had always spooked me when I was a teenager, slipping in past curfew, smelling of cigarettes and occasionally a boy's too-strong cologne. I was giddy, then, and extra sensitized to being caught with kisses blushing from my cheeks, moon-mad with night activity, the scent of whiskey caught up in my hair.

Father had demanded to be placed in his study after the doctors told us that there wouldn't be a next August. We'd hired a day nurse to dole out meals and pills (which for the most part, I assumed he spat out into napkins later). They were all large and neon in hue, all kept in the same tactile orange and white pill containers. The nurse we'd hired had arranged them in a line across my father's desk, each with a sharpied "D" for day and "N" for night. They looked like miniature Easter eggs, which struck me as hilariously sad. I had half a mind to hide them around the house in an effort to spark Father's attention. But I wanted him happy, even if it shortened his life. Father was never one to hope for a lost cause.

"If I'm around my books, and I have you, dear child, to talk with, I don't give a damn about reaching seventy."

He would be seventy next month. Daniel and I moved in shortly after the prognosis, setting up residence in my childhood spaces and bumping lives more than we had ever before in the three years of our marriage. We turned my playroom into Daniel's makeshift office. He was a moderately successful children's book author that had the habit of making the most extraordinary messes. I found papers in the bathroom, under the bed, crinkled in shoes, resting in lampshades. It was a strange living condition, one that I constantly felt trapped in by the two men in my life.

Deciding on a glass of warm milk, and a quick check in the study, I opted for the check-in first. Father usually slept through the night. I entered the hallway and came to the white-washed ivory door that held for me all the instances of groundings, scoldings, long nights spent with a book and window thrown open to the katydids and river noises. A figure stood before my father's hospital bed. In the shadows, it amalgamated with the textures of the room, but kept a contiguous form that didn't waver. Like the darkest shade in shadow. I'd forgotten my glasses on the bedside table, so I squinted trying to make out a face, half-convinced the Nyquil I'd taken earlier was messing with me.

It moved to stand at the foot of my father's bed, and bent itself so that both of its palms were pressed against my father's feet.

"Hey! Get away from him."

My voice sounded hoarse. I cleared my throat and walked into the room, striking my toe against the door. I angled myself against the thing. We formed a perfect triangle, and I glanced at my father who was still asleep, one hand thrown back against the pillow in a brutal slant. The figure rose up again, and turned to me. Instead of a face, there was an absence of light. It had the shape and stature of a man. Broad shoulders sloped into strong curves, arms by its side. A wayward nucleus in a dark room. It approached me.

"Who are you?" I asked.

The thing was silent, but also distracted. I felt an intense gaze that I couldn't begin to locate. It stepped closer, and laid a hand on my shoulder. Flinching, I tried to draw back, but my limbs didn't work properly. It drew me towards him in an encompassing embrace.

I felt imaginary, breathless as if I'd just stumbled into

something far deeper than a dream. Little thrills sparked nerves; clouds of mahogany hung over the periphery of my vision. But there was a steady stroke of calm that kept everything at bay. I was drenched by it, soppy and air-light in his touch. It was a gentle crack and diffusion, then I understood that this was far more than physical perimeters; sexuality ceased to exist. It was a percolation of us, a meeting, a conjoining of a negative and positive.

And after what seemed like many hours, it let me go. It was a swoosh, a sudden departing, and it was back at my father's side. I felt cold then and I knew it was time for me to leave. Light had begun outside. I walked over to my father and laid a hand on his scrunched brow. He seemed to sense the warmth of my hand, our presence in his beloved room. I wished his dreams well, bending to kiss him on both cheeks. It didn't seem respectful to cry in Death's presence.

"What have you done?" I asked the darkness and myself.

Its answer took the form of my father's life.

I walked out of my house, then, leaving Death to do his work. I knew in a couple of hours I'd have to feign surprise and grief. I knew, in time, it wouldn't be me faking it. But for the time being, I stepped into the dawn and sat on our big, outdoor porch. I rocked myself and drew my t-shirt closer to me against the chill. It was then that I heard it: haunting, willowy in tenor. It was the wail of a creature, a portentous cry that made my nerves sing. It came from the direction of the large magnolia tree that I'd climbed in as a child, and kissed in as a young woman. I cursed myself again for not thinking of my glasses.

Standing up, I walked out into the lawn to stand just before the great tree. The sound was still in the air, and it began its hymn again, higher-pitched and desperate. I stretched out my hand in offering — a good forty-five degree angle from my body, and willed myself to see the thing.

The whip-poor-will descended from its branch, and settled lightly onto my palm. She had mottled plumage — a mixture of gray and brown. I knew it was a female because her chest lacked the white splotch of a male. Hers was a soft buff that stood out against the black of her throat. She had polished, inky eyes. When she sang again, her short beak opened wide so that I could see the pink of her tongue.

Unconsciousness returned, and I was shifted again from the hospital to the dry, red road where I'd seen the old man. The air was stagnant, and the combination of heat and mud made me sick to my stomach. Here, at least, the thing inside of me was still.

"I don't know what to do, old man," I said.

"You've relied too much on the actions of others to dictate your own."

He was still crouched at the crossroads, and I pushed myself upwards, steadying my weight by spreading my legs a good pace apart.

"If you decide to come with me, you won't come back."

"I know."

"What about your husband?"

"I love him. But I don't know if I can love this thing."

I thought of Daniel: his big, warm hands, the way he'd always, always wanted children. Even before we'd married, he'd talked of our future — beyond the plural of *we* to *us and them*. And I had been alright with these thoughts. They were future plans — vague, scraggly things that I thought about before falling asleep after too much wine. I gently nudged them away — farther and farther — and he had been okay, too, with this. We were young. We had time.

"It is part of you."

"But not of him."

He looked at me. Once again, I saw the milky eye rolling in his joint. It unnerved me. It was like an opalescent moon, a small one — maybe Saturn's — that you rarely give much thought to.

"You have been touched by Death in the living. Are you sure that It is so inviting that you would throw what is yours away?"

"Why did I see him — It — at all?"

"Questions don't account for It. But It always allows a decision."

"How very noble."

I was disgusted, and suddenly quite sick. I vomited, then, into the middle of the road. My insides made a gray splash in the mud. The liquid filled an imprint of my foot that looked like a backwards California.

"It's coming, you know," he said. "The doctors have found a way. And it will be a natural thing. Born of this earth, a woman's belly."

"Nothing's natural about this!"

I choked on a heave, and glared up at him.

"This pain. This senseless pain. I don't even understand how this happened," I said.

"I am not here to answer your questions about life. I am here to guide you across if you so have it."

I turned away from him, heaving again and hating him.

I would have traded this pain for death, gladly.

"She's coming," the doctor said.

He had the type of glasses that reminded me of those NASA scientists you see in textbooks — their rigid mouths sloppy and hung open or occupied by a drooping cigarette, watching their rocket break the atmosphere.

I felt as if she were breaking my own. I clutched the metal railings, legs splayed, the perfect picture of womanhood. There was darkness in every angle of my body. Looking up, I found Daniel's face, framed by the white delivery robe he wore, was jagged; his features seemed out of order somehow. There was no control, only a wild, skittish quality that wracked my body.

"You must keep pushing, Missus. She is very small," said the doctor.

"You must, dear. You're halfway there already," said the nurse.

I was dizzy with drugs and displacement. I could still see the old man with my inner eye, looking on at me calmly, watching life happen with little concern. I pushed and pushed again, straining my neck to look into myself and see.

My child was born on the 28th of July. It died on the 29th.

She was small of frame, like they said. So small, a whole five inches. She had auburn hair and the loveliest of eyes. They were a deep, yawning green that looked black and still in certain lights. She seemed to know us already as she nestled into my arms. I felt as if I were hugging a doll.

Daniel's face was stricken from the moment she finally emerged. I took it for a mixture of relief and surprise, a clap of fatherhood flung on him of sorts. But as I extended my neck with the last bit of strength I could muster, I realized what held his attention, what caused him such horror.

Our child was plainly beaked. Her lips formed a sharp-pointed oval that extended beyond her baby nose into a tight apex. They were not the pink of baby, nor the pale of newborn, but a strange lily-livered yellow that shone with my insides.

LOVE SONG

WE'D BEEN DRINKING for a while, because we called
it a Storm Party. Carol had brought over margarita mix. It was
Tuesday, and I don't think either of us wanted to be alone.
The mix was electric green and powdery, phosphorescent. I
didn't trust it. She'd taken charge of my kitchen, setting up
glasses for the two of us, opening and shutting and reopening
the fridge door. She was spaced out, a little manic in her
desire to serve and be busy. I went into the kitchen and sat
down at the table.

"You okay?" I asked.

"Yeah. Just freaked out, you know? Storms."

She hit the blender button. I waited until its small roar
subsided. There was a clap of thunder, like a far larger echo.

"I like them," I said.

"Why? God, I cannot even deal with that radar blip that
goes off every five minutes on TV."

"Yeah, that's why I mute it."

"But then you can't hear it," she said, turning to look at me. She had a bottle of Milagro Silver in her hand. The liquid glinted in the florescent light and my stomach turned over.

"Hey, I don't really want one of those — I'm just going to have another beer."

"Suit yourself. This is a special recipe, though."

Carol winked at me and showed me the inside of her pocket. There was a packet of powder in a baggie about an inch wide.

"What is that?"

"Just a pick-me-up. Call me generous. Mike is in love with someone else, Lora."

She said all three things like small gunshots, but at the *else* her voice raised and broke off. It sounded sudden and small to me, like a cliff plateauing in symmetrical suicide.

"Oh my God. I'm sorry," I said, because I was sorry, and strange, and shaking. I wondered if it was me he loved. I hoped it was me.

Carol stopped preparing the drinks and I watched her shoulders slump inwards, forming a cage around her heart and breast. I wished she'd turn around so I could see what this type of pain looked like on another human being. The rain kept going, and it seemed even harder, maybe.

"I'll take that with you," I said.

She turned around, then, and looked at me with china blue eyes, smoky with sweat and too much rubbing. Mascara chips clung to her lower lashes.

"Yeah?"

"Yeah."

The thunder came again, and I looked out into my backyard. The sky was pea green, and the trees looked skeletal against it, like large claws, cowed down before an invisible power.

"Our little secret," she said.

She pulled out the baggie and pinched it into our glasses.

"Take it with the marg — it'll mask the taste."

"Cheers," I said, lifting my drink up to bump hers. I caught her face in that moment: serene, focused, with the palest shade of doubt in her features — untraceable, really, if I only looked once.

It tasted like shit, and I swallowed hard, raising my eyes once more to the outside. It was sheet rain, now: the kind that blanketed and grayed out everything.

"You know, I wouldn't mind if one came," she said.

"One what?"

"A tornado. It'd shake things up at least."

I tried to reply, but I felt a wonderful wave of something that made opening my mouth impossible.

"It's Julie. Fucking Julie, from work," she said.

I cleared my throat and reached for a sip of the margarita. It also tasted like shit. She spread out her fingers onto the table, and widened them away from one another. She had child's hands, with little stubby fingers, and crescent-moon fingernails. The ring he'd given her was gone, but I could still see its white ghost circling her finger. I wondered if she could see it too.

"He says he loves me more. *More*. Are we adverbs?"

"I'd much rather be an adjective," I said, tilting a little in my mind. There was a wayward bump and then I settled in. But Julie didn't look a thing like me. I felt myself caving in, and I silently reprimanded myself. This was *Carol's* boyfriend. This was *Carol's* problem.

"Let's go outside and see this. Lora — let's."

"Are you crazy?" I asked, shaking my head, and pulling

away from the periphery of a dream. "It's like hell and brimstone out there."

"Don't tell me you're scared," she said, standing up and gleaming down a smile that looked beautifully crooked.

I had a porch we could sit on, so we took our drinks outside and sat in the damp chairs. I felt the wetness seeping into my shorts and underwear, and I looked out into the storm and felt more centralized. Whatever I'd taken had cast a small fire-lit glow to everything. Even the rain looked on fire. I wondered where Mike was, and where Julie was, and I thought about them being together in the middle of this.

"Emotions are shit," Carol said after a long sip of her drink. She shook her hair out of her face. In that moment she looked alive and frail and angelic — like a half-human, because her skin stretched back into that terrible smile again. I felt my foot go to sleep, and I pushed my way out of the chair and walked to the edge of the porch. I felt the rain slanting inwards. My shirt soon became soaked, but I kept standing there and trying to take in as much feeling as I could possibly hold.

"Without emotion, there'd be no fear, and I could step out into the center of this storm," I said after a while, feeling clever.

"You'd be crazy."

"Yeah, but aren't we *already* crazy with emotion, too?"

"Fair point."

The drug was fast at work on both of us, and Carol hummed something under her breath that sounded like a sad lullaby. She stared into the corner, watching a spider cleave onto its low web. I rocked myself in the chair — my foot angled against the wooden column. I examined my calf, trying to think of the first time I'd ever really noticed Mike. But I couldn't stand that, so I got up once more and leaned against the railing.

And then the sirens went off, and we both looked to the sky. It had stopped raining, and there was a hush that wrapped up everything in the quiet. I looked back at her to make a joke.

"There she is," Carol said, pointing forwards, past me. I looked back and I saw a wedge in the distance, the color of old smoke. The tornado had arrived. Carol got up and came to where I was standing. It was still silent outside, but the wind picked up, and I felt her slow suck, the breeze on my ankles, the guilt that would soon override me.

"Let's go," she said, grabbing my hand and holding on fast. Her eyes were wet and round. I smiled at her, and it felt wonderful, and then I laughed, and she laughed, too. I kissed her on the forehead and whispered, "Fuck him."

We stepped outside and walked out onto my lawn to greet her.

MECHANICS

IT TOOK A WHILE for me to realize I was talking to a robot.

It was his voice that I noticed first — strange and tinny — a male's, presumably white, a pale British intonation that only showed itself in his O's and R's. He punctuated his sentences with incongruous pauses like, "Yes *pause* Miss." I thanked him, accidentally, since thanking a robot seemed a little obtuse in retrospect. He promptly responded, "A piece of *pause* cake."

I laughed, and he asked me to repeat myself. I said never mind.

After hanging up, I smiled. It was more or less one of the pleasantest conversations I'd had in a long time. There was no need for that compulsory aloofness I usually masked my voice in when talking on the phone. I hated phone calls. They made me nervous — not being able to see a face on the other end had always disturbed me. He had been kind, eager to please, even. Straight-laced and endearingly business-like, he was formal in a silly way, like a guy picking up his prom date, being forced to talk to the parents of his crush.

Real conversations made me sweat through my t-shirts so much that there'd be a ring of water under my armpits. My psychiatrist told me I should talk to people, make it an objective, even. But what was the point of a party if you have such a clear-cut agenda? *I'm going to talk to five people tonight.* Who does that? Me, she suggested. Agendas are good for those of us with anxiety disorders.

The next time I call him is about a week later, after I've manually unplugged the Internet, and counted to ten.

Dial three to speak to a representative about trouble-shooting.

And there he is — his voice makes my blood firecracker in my veins. I feel faint, and realize with blooming chagrin that I'm swooning.

"How may I help you?"

"My Internet's out."

He walks me through the steps I know by heart — unplugging certain cords, re-kindling a connectivity that I want lost for a couple more minutes.

"Is that all you need today, Miss?"

There's that adorable pause again, punctuating his words into clear, staccato clips.

"What's your name?" I say in a moment of love-fueled clarity.

"My name is John, Miss."

"Call me Clara."

"Miss Clara."

I love the way he says it. A soft "A", a curdling of the — CL.

"Can I call you sometime?" I ask.

"Our services are open 24-7, with tech support on weekends."

That's a yes if I've ever heard one.

On Monday, I tell my psychiatrist that I've met someone. She's excited for me, in that restrained way of hers — tight, gummy smile, a boundary of sorts between her peach lipstick and pale, hairless upper-lip. She looks at me with goldfish eyes; today, I don't care. I'm a woman in love.

I call once a week in the beginning, but it's a speedy type of tenderness, gnawing at my mind. I begin counting the moments like shiny coins, bartering with myself about the actuality of our affair. I go through the proper stages: disbelief, a longing that stretches the skin, like a tent around my heart, and then the subsequent call, the reassurance of him as a tenable entity.

He fixes me, and I spill out love words with uncorked fervor. I confuse him, I know, but it doesn't stop me, or him, from always, always answering.

It's the fifth week, and a Monday. The rain has stopped; now there's only a mugginess that creeps in under my doorframe, into my teacup, infecting my lemon. I decide to call John.

I go through the usual numbers, an anticipation welling in my pits.

"Hello, this is Andy with the tech team. How can I help you today?"

"Where's John?"

"John? Oh — you mean our answer-bot? He had a bug

in his system. You know how that sort of stuff goes — more of an experiment, really. Glad too — you know, I lost work hours with that damned recording service anyways. Hoping headquarters'll just do away with the whole project entirely."

"Whole project?"

His voice rubs against my ear. I can feel its wrongness.

"Yeah — with the recorded voice. It kind of put customers off, talking with something that, you know, doesn't really live or breathe or think. Anyways, how can I help you today? Internet trouble?"

I don't call back for weeks. I've stopped seeing my psychiatrist. She calls me a few times at first, leaving me short voicemails that sound concerned, almost wounded.

Call me back, Clara. Call me back.

Finally, she stops like everyone else does. The thing is: you have to work to be loved and remembered. Once you stop that, it's only a matter of time before your memory fades like yellowed paper.

But all I do is imagine John saying these words to me: I love you, I miss you, Clara, Clara, Clara, over and over again like Technicolor waves, dashing the static and impossibility of a silence as small and silver as the moon.

THE HOUSE HUNTERS

IT WAS ONE OF THOSE bleak March days when the earth wore a perpetual frown, blackened and charred into the ground. The melting snow had the consistency of shoe polish, mixed as it was with the grime of footprints, broken leaves, and mud. Henry thought the winter trees looked like black staples. He looked at his wife, Luna. She wore the same tight-lipped expression she had worn all morning — rigged up at the corners like two competing commas.

"Want some coffee?" He nudged his paper cup out to her, watching the steam form a boundary between their faces in the cold.

"No, Henry, I *do not* want any coffee."

They continued up the mild slope, slipping occasionally on the wet ground. The leftover snow made satisfying cracks under his feet like those small poppers that kids threw on the ground or at relatives on Fourth of July evenings.

"Well, it's there," he said, pointing to a small clearing of dead grass.

Last month, there'd been a graveyard sale. After his first heart attack back in the fall, Henry had taken the sale as a sort of cosmic sign. At some point, death becomes just another business transaction.

"The Roberts have one under a tree," said Luna.

"I don't want acorns falling on me when I'm grappling with eternal sleep," Henry said.

"It's just so..." Luna shrugged her shoulders. She was a small woman who never seemed to take up much space; she kept her hair cropped close to her ears. She was pixie-like despite her seventy years, two children, and fondness for Daschunds.

"I think it's non-refundable. Since it was on sale and all," Henry said, looking at his wife with mild irritation.

"It's fine, I guess. The Clemsons said theirs is big enough for the kids, too."

"The Clemsons are pretentious."

"Yeah, but wouldn't it be nice to have Johnny and Sarah near us?"

"Unless they get a divorce. Then, that'd just be awkward."

Luna smiled. "How much was this again?"

"Five hundred. We had the option of monthly maintenance but that was an extra seventy and I didn't bring the checkbook."

"The kids can do it."

"Picnics with Grandma and Grandpa every Saturday. They won't have to pack too many sandwiches; that's a plus. Say, I wonder what my cravings will be like when I'm dead. Will I still hate olives?"

"You're awful," Luna said, tugging a tiny spike of gray behind her ear — a girlish gesture she'd never been able to shake despite numerous hairstyles, varying lengths.

"No, really. Hear me out — what're we going to do all day? Should I pack reading materials?"

"You're ridiculous. They wouldn't let you take your library to the grave."

"People've taken weirder things. And why not? It's my damn grave, it's paid for."

"Wouldn't fit."

"So I'd take a few of the classics. Nothing too highbrow, of course. Don't want to make enemies with the neighbors."

"I could take my pottery, I guess," Luna said, thoughtfully.

"Of course you could."

"But the foot pedal and all wouldn't fit."

"Luna dear, I think death is far less literal than you think it is."

"It's the most literal thing there is."

Henry eased himself to the ground, crossing his legs and remembering a vague childhood satisfaction that went along with it. His joints ached. He needed a cigarette. He looked at his wife to join him. She sat too, straightening her legs out before her, neatly tucking the folds of her taffeta Sunday dress like fancy restaurant napkins.

"Never knew house hunting could be as simple as this," he said.

"Mortgage free. What'll happen to the car?"

They both looked in the direction of their '05 Honda, electric blue because Luna said it made her feel young when she drove it.

"We aren't supposed to worry about that kind of stuff," he said, placing his hand on her knee and feeling its bony imprint.

"What about Oscar? Why didn't we get him a place, too?"

Henry regretted not thinking about their dead and buried

dog. He'd been an old fellow, stiff-legged, squat, graying on the tops of his ears in a decidedly distinguished fashion.

"Can you relocate graves like that?"

"I don't know," she said. "I don't think I'd want to see what came out of the earth."

Henry looked at their plot of space once more. The day was cold — in the rigid kind of way that only Southern winters afford, righteous in its weather. Henry shrugged his jacket closer to him.

"We'll make it home, though," Henry said, after a while. He had been thinking about a good many things — about the space underground, the smell, what blazer he'd like to wear for the afterlife, if there happened to be one of those. Henry had always liked to come prepared for parties, and he wasn't about to slack off now.

He looked over to ask for her opinion, and saw that Luna was crying. Her mittened hands were pressed up against the top half of her face. Her skin was pale blue, and the tip of her nose was as red as a maraschino cherry.

"Oh, honey, it'll be alright," he said, bringing his arm around her small shoulders and tugging her into his embrace. "I won't bring all the books. There'll be room. And you should wear that nice violet number I've always liked you in."

Luna raised her face and looked at her husband for a long moment.

"The one with the lace trim on the hem?" she asked.

"That one! You wore it a few Christmases back."

"And maybe with my cloche hat," she said. "Yes, I think the hat'll do nicely."

He nestled her again, like he used to do when they were young and still discovering things. He breathed in the scent of wet snow and the same perfume she'd worn for thirty years.

"Say — so what're we bringing again? Let's start from the beginning."

PLAYTIME

SOMEHOW, FROM A DREAM that shared its particulars with reality, I ended up here. It's chintzy; cozy in the sort of way grandmothers would appreciate with porcelain bunnies and thick carpeting. There's a large, salmon-pink sofa to the left of me, backed against the wood-paneled walls with an aureate design of petals among pearlescent fronds. I can't decide which petal belongs to which plant — but they are all together, bloomed out and almost, I think, carnal. Stalks strangle bulbs sweetly, as if they are lovers. But it's messy, too, the scene and fuss they make of the furniture. I avert my eyes.

She comes to me before long, measuring about a foot and a half tall — she reaches my knee, and plants herself firmly before me, unafraid and terribly beautiful. With every movement, I hear a "click" that locks itself securely in her tiny joints. There is something mechanical within her movement, meditated and concise. It's a cursory sort of pleasure that forms the crook of her smile.

"Welcome," she says, crossing her legs together and

plopping her cloth bottom smack against the floor. "You're here to play?"

She fiddles with a strand of cottony hair the width of a finger. My finger.

"I was hoping you'd tell me," I finally say, peripherally realizing that we aren't the only things in the room.

There are others, playthings. They are gleaming, jewel-toned in the tepid light of the living room. Shiny coats and painted-on grins that lack the wholesome quality I remember in my own possessions; a grimace, a shuffle of plastic and metal against wood. The changes disturb me, reprimand my humanity. And I feel their eyes on the inches of my skin like night spiders — those plastic, curious eyes that feel impertinent. I don't begrudge a dream if that's all this is. And I want to shed my skin, climb out of myself and look back over the soul's shoulder to see what they see. I am the outsider, I realize, faintly, before I black out.

I sit up straight, hair mussed into my eyelashes so that I have to sweep a dark curl away from my nose in order to see anything. The doll-girl is standing at the foot of the couch and drumming her tiny, left hand on the cushion. Her stitched eyes are as wide and dark as sunflowers. Each lash is meticulously formed like a baby's finger bones. Her prominent cheeks are perfect circles of rose. She doesn't smile. I can sense an expectancy that chides me into speech.

"Where exactly am I?"

"You're in the playhouse. Are you ready to play?"

"But how long was I asleep?" I gesture towards the couch, conscious of her all-too-obvious impatience.

"We don't keep clocks here. But we did get bored waiting on you."

Before I have time to answer, a knobby figure appears from behind a chair. He resembles a marionette, and taller than the doll. I can make out where his limbs are attached by screws — they glisten in the crook of his elbows, the notch of his knees. To walk, he takes tentative steps forward, bending the base leg so that he can stretch out the other, searching for solid earth like a foundling astronaut.

"This is Cho," says the doll-girl, "and I'm Lina." The second introduction is an afterthought. She seems puzzled by the necessity of the action, but goes through it just the same, childlike and dutiful.

We decide on a game of checkers. I glance at Cho, curious. He seems content with the silence. He moves awkwardly, but seems accustomed to his artless limbs and unbothered by his physicality, like a child who's yet to learn self-consciousness. The checkers are the correct size for a human, but Cho and Lina struggle with the chips, which measure the expanse of their hands. They look more like small saucers in their palms. I offer my help, and I get a glare from Lina. Pride, it seems, still clings to the smallest of us.

I let them win, and win again, and after the second game I raise my eyes into Cho's wooden robin blue. He looks at me with pallid observation. I stare back, and finally, he turns his head back to Lina.

"Let's do something else," he says.

"But what else? It's usually one game and then they go back there," she says. Her voice is salient, sharp.

"We should probably clean up," she adds when he fails to answer.

I smooth my finger over my cuticles and then reexamine them like seashells. They are pink against my chalky flesh, and I am only more reminded of my place here. Or lack of it. I miss the feel of flesh against meat. I feel myself being touched, look up, and see Cho very near to me, resting his wooden hand on my upper arm.

"Play, Lady?"

"Of course."

There are no other words because at once I see a narrow weight in his body — his limited face, his untethered physicality around me that quivers and responds to my every motion. I could lose myself in this assurance of place.

"Cho, I think she should go now. Go wait. Do something."

"You never let them stay! We hardly get to know them."

He pivots to where he faces Lina. By her expression, I can tell this sort of confrontation is a rare thing. I begin edging away, in hopes that this will all disappear. But his tiny grip tightens, and I'm held, then, by a longing and empathy I cannot fully realize.

"She stays," he says.

"Okay then, she stays."

And I, the object I am, stay put.

We shoot the breeze — me, apprehensive, my legs tucked tightly underneath myself. With Cho's hand gripping me in firm possessiveness, I am still and unable. Possessed fully, and objectified. Lina clips her sentences, which are usually just answers to my observations. Cho asks me questions about things he's heard from their other visitors.

Have I had scrambled eggs?

Is there really such a thing as the moon?

Is there a man in it?

With each of my answers, he dips his head for a moment. His mouth opens a little, and he bobs there, thinking or absorbing, until he's satisfied.

"Where are the others?" I ask.

"Oh, they're here. We don't play that often. They forget a lot," Lina says.

"What do you mean forget?"

Instead of answering, she stands up, so trim and fair, more a reed than a figure. Her lacy clothes swathe her petite figure and never seem to rumple. My fear for her ceases as she turns her back to me. She looks like my own doll stuffed away in an attic somewhere, bitten by dust. She stands straight and whistles. It's alarming and clear. For a few seconds, there's only the silence.

"Come out, come out, wherever you are."

And they do come, timidly rushed. A stuffed giraffe with the platonic smile I remember from childhood; a bemused jack-in-the-box, his mouth a horseshoe of a grin; a tiny ballerina, her toes barely skimming the floor and winking with pink; a seasoned army man with posture like a board.

They are called to attention before me. I clasp my hands together in front of me, amazed.

"Meet the mistress," is all Lina says.

I feel the scoff, the superiority she feels towards my human form. I introduce myself with a hopeful smile, a fleeting sunset wave of my hand. And they nod back, and then there's silence, and I crumple my hands together with anxiety.

"She's different than the others," says the Jack, finally. He has ombre eyes, and his skin is polished a steady pearl.

"Taller, bigger."

"Yes, she's older than the usual ones," Lina replies. "And more troublesome."

"And pretty, too," offers the ballerina.

"But what will He say?" asks the tiny soldier. His voice is more squeak than baritone.

"He?" I look to Lina and Cho. Their faces are impassive.

"He won't be back for a good while," Lina finally says, looking at me with uncanny speculation.

Days go by. I long to see a clock face — by now, it seems like an old friend. Time isn't of the essence here. She's not a necessary marker for activity and non-activity, and she stretches herself out like a roasting, endless summertime. But the rest of my companions are content, or at least oblivious to the lack of chronology. There are games — perpetual and deeply constant. The art of Game is the fixture in these things' lives like religion is in others'. My head feels swollen with rules and double-rulings and gamey catch-phrases and check mates. I tire easily, and am never hungry anymore. No one eats, besides pretending with the play food made of thick plastic, the rubber grapes I pinch between forefinger and thumb, idly; sometimes I lay myself down onto the plush carpet and run my fingers through the tendrils like grass. No dust, or tracked-in bits of outside from soles of shoes; we are in states of constant doldrums, staleness that dulls the appetite, but never satisfies.

One day or an hour or a week later, I wake from one of my now dreamless naps. I've found that dreaming here is impossible. I am either conscious or blacked out. There is no latent sleepiness, because the idea of sleep has lost its comfort. It's now, simply, the retreat I go to unwillingly when there are no games to play.

Recently, Cho has been sitting with me for large portions of time. I've begun the process of forgetting. It's slow, so I'm not afraid, but merely curious about my own retreating understanding of a world I once knew all too well. I can still see the faint outlines of my mother and father. My mother, with dried paint under the nails: they were slight, blue-blooded hands.

Cho's memory begins not on a specific day, but at the moment he looked up into his creator's face.

"Gep," he calls him, "short for 'Gepetto.'"

I nod, asking Cho about Him. I alter my voice to match the reverence accorded to this mysterious figure.

"He's like the other humans, but the oldest we've ever known. He is tall with white hair and sea eyes. He has whiskers," and Cho rubs the length of his chin and grins at me proudly.

"I asked him to paint some on me, but he said I'd look silly. Lina agreed."

We both turn our faces Lina's way. She is sitting, both perfectly shaped legs spread in front of her, examining a marble. She looks into it like some sort of wishing glass; her pretty nose occasionally bumps against its solid surface.

"And Lina? She's all boss," I say.

As always, Cho merely shrugs, moot on the subject of Lina.

"Are you afraid she'll hear?" I say under my breath, nudging him with a gentle hand. I'm still surprised by his woodenness.

Cho turns to me then, meeting my gaze, a look that causes me to blink away to my knees.

"Because of Him," he replies. "Because He may hear," he says, his usually bright, falsetto voice is low and black. He jabs my ribs with an acicular finger, and nods.

"Ow!"

"You humans are terribly sensitive," he says, a mixture of envy and doubt etched into the wooden grooves of his boyish face.

"But what about your creator?" he asks, shifting his tone to convivial once more.

"What about them?"

"Them?"

"Yeah, my parents. I guess you could say I have two creators."

"But how is that?"

"Well, they met. And liked each other enough to stay together and experiment with me."

I shrug it off, slightly embarrassed about the subject matter he's accidentally stumbled on.

"Tell me about them."

"I told you, it's hard to remember specifics these days."

"Try, Lady. Tell me a story."

I look at Cho, then. Really actually look at the shape of his eyes and the way his deep dimples are etched into his cheeks.

"She modeled engagement rings for a jeweler. It's a guy who makes these lovely stones and minerals into, well, ornaments. Like this!" I hold out my wrist to show him the sliver of golden band.

"My father, engaged to another woman, saw one of her advertisements in a magazine, and fell in love with the idea of her hands. He drew out his savings and headed to the store to purchase the ring for the woman he was to marry. My mother wasn't there, but the ring still was. Purchased, and proposing again, my father slipped off the former white diamond, and tugged the emerald Chantilly ring onto the woman's finger. It hadn't looked the same. Knowing he had to find the woman with the right hand, he ended the engagement and set out in search for my mother."

"In search for beauty," Cho says.

It's a simple way of putting the notion, but I can't deny

it. I'd always been bothered by that story, despite the neat loveliness and tidy ending. He was, in his own way, in search for an ideal. And who can blame a guy in search of perfection? Then, and only then, could there be that type of wonderful, but chimerical love.

"And my favorite color came out being green," I say.

After a stream of more games and more chatter, a door opens and then closes from the other room. Everything stops, then, all eyes transfixed in the direction of the sound, and then a sudden shifting to Lina, who, though still self-possessed, orders a retreat.

Toys scatter to all sides of the room. A massive evacuation, and I sit dumbly in the middle, too shocked to ask where my destination should be.

"Girl, get up and brush yourself off. You're about to meet our maker," orders Lina, leaning into my ear, and tugging on a lank curl.

I scramble up, straightening my jeans and blowzy shirt that is crumpled from the hours and days spent lounging on the carpet. I tug my hair behind my ears, and wipe a sheen of perspiration from my upper lip. I haven't seen a mirror, only brief glimpses of recognition in the bases of brass lamps and cold, reflecting eyes.

Our door opens, and a man steps into the room. I feel the hush on the hairs of my arms. A breeze, a sigh, the room seems altogether foreign and sticky with use.

"Seems we have a visitor, Lina," says the man, who very much resembles the man Cho described: tall, with a shock of white hair that swirls like cream into a perfect curve. He wears glasses that do nothing to hide the beryl shine of his eyes.

"I'm..." I stammer, foolishly holding out a sweaty palm

95

for a shake.

"No matter, no matter." He waves it away.

"I'm Gepetto," he says, and I realize that he's wearing a cape of deep maroon. It looks watery in the artificial light — velvet, grand, a little absurd.

"The place smells of her," he says to Lina.

"And Cho, it seems you've finally found that..." he pauses to look my way with an appraising nod, "fair maiden, and, dare I say, romance? Too many story books make for a naughty boy, Cho."

Cho ducks his chin into his wooden chest, quickly releasing his hand from mine. The man beams, pleased with this unhappiness he's caused so casually.

I look from Cho to Gepetto.

"My dear girl, I am in the toy business as you can see."

Gepetto offers me a large hand. I hesitate, looking back to Lina who refuses to meet my gaze. Cho has turned himself completely away by now, against the wall as if acting the class fool.

I give Gepetto my hand, and he leads me into the dark room.

It's a deep navy in here, and far colder than in the living room. My steps sound hollow and yawning, and the man's grasp is so light on my hand that his fingers tickle the middle of my palm. He lets go to make a few attempts at lighting a match, and finally, a flare bursts through the darkness. The candlestick he holds is twice as large and twice as thick as a regular one. There's a glass flame constructed to emulate the licking of fire. I look beyond it, and see a room filled with material — metal, copper, tin, brass, wood — oh, so much wood with serrated edges, fir, oak, walnut, and an array of hemlocks against three slabs of purplelock and sweetgum and a lovely piece of willow. There are paints: deep burgundy, sunrise orange, and shades of beige and blue; I spot the exact color of Lina's cheeks, and my stomach somersaults.

"Every creator needs the right supplies."

"It's marvelous," I say, feeling a compliment is necessary. I fight the bile stuck like hot glue in my throat.

He inclines his head to me in acknowledgment.

"And, well — how do you animate them?" I ask, finally voicing the only question I care about. "I mean, is it — is it batteries? Or some new sort of robotics?"

"A combination of many things, of years of work, of the right wood and screw and bolt and..." he considers me then, "person."

I nod, finally understanding. For the first time in ages, I'm lent purpose, and I think back to the beautiful green of my mother's ring, the glint of metal and stone.

"So you know what's next, clever girl?"

Again, he guns me that clear, gripped gaze of his that is so blue it's almost obscene.

"I believe so."

Memory is a transient thing, fickle, even. But I believe in my memories as I do in the varnish on my skin, the turtle green of my glossy eyes, the way I wind up so precisely in the back — which Cho usually helps me with, gentle and firm because even though we are items, things, there's always the capacity for love between the misplaced.

I do not know what to call this place; I never will. A go-between of sorts, a cleft in the universe that was overlooked, a glitch in my own memory, even. Who knows what our pasts are, so cut off from the on-going reality that fails to look backwards, rarely forwards, and always, always, demanding of the exigent now.

But our purpose is to play — and keep on playing and playing, pretending at these little, sea-combed lives, maintaining one endearment: our wear and tear.

X

THE TRIP

HER FATHER HAD ALWAYS been solitary. He accepted his condition not with bravery, but with a reasonableness that anchored her beliefs in a reluctant, steady present that she could not escape. He was dying, and everyone agreed that the best thing to do was make a lot of food.

Her mother baked non-stop. Loretta would wake up in the middle of the night, rubbing dreams from her eyes, and stumble into a bright, yellow kitchen that smelled of heated sugar. Her mother poured tears into her bread puddings, sighs into her muffins; there was a brooding, sturdy quality that quietly infected the house.

Her father became distant; he stayed up late, an inky outline against the blue of the television that bathed the living room in underwater waves. *Undulating.* She remembered that word from high school vocabulary tests. She'd come in sometimes to look at him as he slept in his recliner — the room spilled shadows onto his face, but it was peaceful, almost entirely blank. She divided up life into *then* and *now*, because his face changed again in the mornings — reestablishing itself into watchful eyes, a tight mouth that looked as if it had never known a smile.

It was time to go ballooning.

His doctors suggested it first, with guilty eyes, and trepid, kind words that they'd practiced in bathroom mirrors, not in school: *let-down words*, words that said things in the spaces. Ballooning was a last-stop kind of thing. It meant that the medicine didn't matter, that it was time to take some action before it was too late. Thanks to insurance, the lessons and balloon costs were fully covered. Hospitals everywhere encouraged families to take this time to learn together, to practice the mantra of teamwork, which was supposed to bring out the best in everyone. Loretta's mother, however, had a phobia of heights. Roller coasters were not an option; even airplane rides required large amounts of sedation. But Loretta had quit college recently, after failing an English seminar twice and being caught with whiskey in her handbag, and a pocketknife stuck deep into the claret core of a grapefruit like a pincushion. She had nothing better to do than explore the sky.

Their first training session happened a week later. In the beginning, there'd been a guide that went along with the patient's explorations. But after a few years of this, statistics showed that learning the craft for themselves actually increased patient satisfaction. Now, it was up to the patient (and their respective families) to learn.

"I don't want to do this," her father told their trainer.

The young man smiled at Loretta — a side-glance of sorts that looked like a plea for help. She didn't give him any reassurance. He had hair-colored hair and a nondescript smudge of a face. He looked, she thought, like a boy.

Instead of responding, he cheerily said, "So the first thing we're learning today is how to steer. Are you familiar with sailboats, sir?" He directed his joker's grin towards her father.

"No. I like staying on the *ground*."

"Well, that's okay. As long as you have a willing attitude, it's a piece of cake. By the way, let's call each other by our firsts — I'm Timothy."

He looked around at them, gave a curt nod, and angled his clipboard towards the sky.

"Okay, so first we're going to go over the logistics of the propane valve. It's just like turning the kitchen stove on. This knob here —" Timothy pointed to a small, red handle underneath a mass of machinery the size of two heads, "you turn it, and the gas flow increases. This is how you control your *vertical* speed. For a big shot up, you turn it quickly and high — a smaller, more even-paced ascent requires slow turning."

He made Loretta and her father practice turning the knob slowly at first, but after a while, Loretta grew bored and yanked it to full blast. A large flame exploded from the propane valve. Heat bounced off her cheeks. Her father smiled, and Loretta smiled back at him, while Timothy started, slapping her hand away and turning it completely off.

"Enough of that. Next — there's the 'chute."

He pointed ten feet away from where they stood. The balloon's envelope was huge, lying mole-hill-high in welts on the ground in green and purple nylon.

"See, here we have the *gore*," said Timothy. His pronunciation made it sound like two syllables. "It's sewn in these long panels. You'll be able to really see it once we fire'er up next week."

Loretta thought it looked like one of those deflated jumping gyms. Her father stared at his hands, and the wind picked up so that the enveloped dipped and tucked in rhythm to the elements.

"Now, I want you to read over these handouts this weekend, and be ready for notes on Monday. There's diagrams on page three."

Her mother had taken over the kitchen. The thing was, her constant culinary exploits would've been welcome to Loretta if her mother had actually known how to cook. Instead, it was cream-filled brioches, spoilt and sagging; irrevocably bent croissants; calzones with pepperoni and olives with the pits still inside, forgotten, pruny, enmeshed in burnt cheese. They ate her food without words, while her mother didn't touch the three courses she'd prepared; instead, she watched her family with intent, dark blisters for eyes.

"So how was it?"

"It was fine," Loretta said, answering for her father. "Informative, I guess."

"What'd you learn?"

"How to turn a goddamn lever like goddamn chimpanzees."

He'd said this to his food, and Loretta saw a weariness cross her mother's face.

"Next week, it's about the actual balloon part."

"Really honey? That's nice," her mother said, staring ahead into their great backyard, the windows a composite of fulgent light.

"You're lucky. The only real problems people run into is at the beginning and end of their flights," said Timothy.

It was Tuesday morning, bright for so early. It had rained overnight and the grass was cool and wet; their shoes crunched, and Loretta stepped on a mushroom. Its sinewy insides spilled onto the grass, and she felt a tight little jerk in her throat.

"So I'm going to need your help with setting it up. Takes more than one pair of hands. That's why we suggest *whole* families participate," Timothy said, looking at Loretta and her father with disapproving consternation.

"First things first, we're attaching the burner to the basket."

He had them lug the envelope out of its protective covering and spread it gently across the grass. Their lawn was large enough for three of them. A few curious squirrels edged towards it, sniffing with their black beaded noses, flickering tails. One of the perks of being country folks, she guessed, was a hell of a lot of room.

After spreading it out like a circus tent and catching their breath, Timothy started the massive fan that had been brought over by two men in a pick-up truck. Both had sucked at their cigarettes as they'd jostled it to the ground, turned on their heels, and left without a word. Their faces looked raw underneath their bandanas, like once-wet mud.

Timothy started the fan, and it roared.

"Don't stand in front of it, or it might blow someone as small as you away," Timothy said into her ear. He'd appeared by her side with a quick, sidelong step. He feigned covering his ears in pain, and then touched her elbow knowingly. She smiled, not quite meeting his eyes but instead fixing them on the pink outline of a zit that was forming just below his top layer of chin skin.

"There?" she said, swiping her index finger along it, as if flicking away a fly. His cheeks turned red, and he moved away from her, taking out his notepad to give something an emphatic strike on paper.

Once the balloon resembled a poached egg, Timothy shut off the fan and blasted the burner into the envelope's mouth. Loretta was surprised by how quickly it righted itself.

"Okay, I'm going to need one person to stay here to help me steady this thing. Mr. Pierce, you want to get in the basket now? Just sit down in it — you'll be able to stand shortly. Basket's tied to the stake so it won't rise up more than five feet at the most."

Her father, a primarily indoors-and-work-study man, who was helpless in all this action, surprised Loretta by walking over to the basket and climbing in, drawing his knees to his chest, and staring fixedly ahead into the balloon's hot cave.

"Loretta, come over here and hold this girl steady so she won't go vertical too quickly. It's going to tug a little."

She followed his orders, pushing down onto the wicker basket. They waited around five minutes, letting it fully rise like some sort of large, luminous green bread dough, and all the while, the basket became more and more difficult to keep horizontal.

"Okay. On the count of three. We're gonna let her go. One, two, three."

Loretta let go and in one fluid swoop the balloon righted itself and began to rise, straining against the rope like a dog.

"Mr. Pierce! Fire one steady stream from the burner. Just pull for a few seconds! Show 'er who's boss!"

Loretta could see her father grasp for the lever. He looked down at them with wild, caged eyes. His moustache was mussed and she could make out the outline of a green vein in his forehead that splayed itself against his thin skin like a snake. He tugged, and fire shot from the burner, righting everything. He looked down at them once more, and his eyes were wet. Then, he looked past hers, and she turned.

"Timothy, stay for dinner, won't you?"

Her mother was standing behind them, taking in the scene and twisting a gingham dishcloth in her hands.

They had dinner outside with the mess of newborn mosquitoes and ripening dark. Her mother had made a pot roast, despite the summer temperatures. Loretta speared a solid block of potato with her fork. Timothy was on his second helping. Loretta had always studied the way people ate, as if there was an algorithm hidden in side dishes. Timothy laid his carrots out in a neat row on his plate. He halved each carrot, chose a side, and slipped it into his mouth.

"So we'll be able to launch you folks in the next week or so," he said, after chewing a bite with relish.

"Oh, that's wonderful," her mother said, laying down her spoon, looking at each of them with a ready expression. It always seemed to be that — ready. Never chosen, hardly transfixed, but receptive and open to the wayward mass before her. Maybe that's what mothers did best, she thought. Readied things.

"Who wants a drink?" asked Loretta.

"Loretta, it's a Wednesday for God's sake," her mother said, picking up her spoon once more, stirring the brown sludge into browner sludge. She put it down again, angling it away from the white napkin.

"Loretta got caught drinking at school."

"Well, she's a teenager after all," Timothy said, dicing another carrot.

"Actually, I'm twenty. Late bloomer, you know?"

She didn't need or want Timothy's pathetic attempts at

defending her honor at her own dinner table. She looked to her father.

"Daddy, you told me once that you were drinking at fifteen. When you went fishing and swimming at the creek with Mr. Timbers."

"Not now, Loretta," her father said, glancing up for the first time all evening. The sickness had made his skin look like paper. Beautiful paper, but paper, still, with the tiniest of wrinkles that looked like silver glitches in an otherwise solid snow. Paper you wouldn't dare to write on at all.

"But he also didn't have the opportunity for *university*," her mother hissed.

Loretta looked back to her father, and then met Timothy's gaze.

"Full scholarship. She was so bright."

"Is bright," Loretta corrected. "I'm still alive, and I'm still sitting at your dinner table."

But it was too late, and she knew it, and had known it since she'd gotten dropped off in a taxi months back. She had failed at something too large and too weighty and now she was here, and explanations were a moot point.

Loretta was charged with walking Timothy to his car. Gender roles had been reversed, apparently, or maybe it was because they were young, and firmly lumped into a category they weren't sure how to share. They walked in silence, nothing companionable, but remote and heavy, and she walked faster than he did, skimming the surface with her sneakers, in trepidation for her walk back to a home that no longer seemed familiar.

"You're brave to go up there by yourself," Timothy said to her back.

"I won't be alone; I'll be with my dad."

"Yeah, but most kids are leery of this sort of thing."

"I've got nothing better to do," she said, turning to face him, surprised by his closeness. It was dim, and she couldn't make out his expression, which she assumed was infuriating.

"Of course you do. You're so young."

She shrugged, wiping her forehead with her hand and gathering the warm sweat that had collected on it like silk.

"And very beautiful," he added.

"Is this what you do? Help old men fly balloons and sleep with their daughters as payment?"

"Not exactly. But I won't deny I have a number."

"You're disgusting."

"No, just good at my job. I've made my career in helping men and women run away from death."

"They're not running away from it."

"Yes they are. We all are. Every second we're running from it with all our might, as fast as our legs can carry us. Balloons are the ultimate distraction from the inevitable. "

Loretta was silent. The inevitable. It was such a strong, proud word. It clipped at your tongue, a five-dollar word, probably, at any local spelling bee.

"So what happened with you?" he asked.

"You already know, don't you? You were sitting right there at the table."

"I heard a disappointed parent's account."

Loretta wasn't sure if it was a good idea to continue this conversation, but Timothy was the first person who'd asked and she was so very, very tired, suddenly.

"I drank a lot and decided I didn't like school as much as I thought I would."

"So you aren't going back?"

"Probably not. I think there're other things I want to do more. Like live with my parents. Like fly a balloon. And watch my father die."

"The inevitable," he said.

"Yes, I suppose. Head towards the inevitable," she said, wringing her left hand with her right, and looking into the starlight.

The day of the launch was cloudy, but the breeze was good: a genial wind, balmy and encouraging. The trees surrounding their enormous backyard were mint green, all woken up for a spring that Loretta and her father would miss. They had set no return date, which was unusual. Her father had merely shrugged, saying they'd do what felt right at the moment. They'd learned how to land, and had a list of "outlets" that kept travel foods in stock, along rocky shores and mountain ranges. Loretta's mother had baked several questionable pastries the night before, setting them out like trophies on their kitchen table. Cherry-checkered cloth, neat, white napkins doubled into crisp borders that looked like snowy, jagged mountains; it was an imperfect picture of hurried domesticity. Her mother's eyes were luminous, plate-sized things that took in every detail. A manic energy pervaded her quick, hen-like movements behind the stove, even in the way she tucked her hair, undone and graying, behind her ears.

Loretta walked outside; she hadn't seen her father all morning. Humidity enveloped her bare shoulders, and she wondered what she should do with her hair. It was long and thick, but took to tangling and matting like troublesome weeds. She took a bit between her fingers and rubbed the strands together, mussing it into a dark knot.

Her father was in the basket poring over maps, his reading glasses perched on top of his head. He needed glasses, and he had glasses, but he never wore them to read. They were always only close by, within a moment's reach on his lap, balanced on his head, there and ready but forgotten.

"You decide where you want to go?" she asked, settling in beside him on the ground. The basket was nine feet long and wide, plenty of room for two rolled-up sleeping bags, a small stash of food, and water.

"I've got ideas. What about you?"

"Anywhere and everywhere."

"Attagirl."

A rare smile, those small, square teeth that had yellowed. His eyes were lake-colored this morning, which was good.

"What's something you've always wanted to do?"

"What do you mean?"

"Like a bucket list."

"Well," her father looked towards the ground, squinting. "I've always wanted to sleep with Barbara Streisand."

"Wait, what? Are you kidding me?"

"I mean it, kid. That hair of hers, that little nose...."

"I meant something not earth-shattering to your only child's psyche."

Her father grinned. "I don't know. There were lots of things. Now, I'm flying. It's air we're talking about. The most powerful stuff there is."

Timothy showed up around noon with a group of men that would help launch them. They'd already packed the non-perishables, a dozen canteens of ice water, her father's supply of pills, Loretta's birth control (just for normalcy's sake), a wireless phone charger, a pack of matches, and a stack of paperbacks.

A meteor-psychic came too, showing up in a shiny black car that looked more beetle than machine. She was young, with hair the color of wheat balled back in one of those effortlessly chic buns that Loretta had seen in French magazines. Meteor-psychics usually weren't taken all that seriously; they were the seers of the weather business, persons who claimed to have an inner eye for Mother Nature's mysterious ways, who understood the wind on a fundamental level that disbarred all science and theory.

"Protocol," she blushed as her excuse. "I'm here to read the weather."

She apparently knew Timothy and didn't think much of him; her face stiffened, and Loretta could see the make-up lines that traced a smooth curve down her chin.

"I'll just get set up over here," she explained, walking away with quick, nipping steps. Loretta followed her.

"So how do you predict the weather, exactly?"

"It's actually really simple, if you have the touch."

"Which you do?"

"Yes. It's a generational thing. The meteorologists use us all the time, otherwise they wouldn't know which way the wind blew. Idiots."

She showed Loretta a special gel that she dipped her finger into.

"It over-sensitizes the nerves in the finger. So, here, I dip my pointer finger in like that, make sure it's good and rubbed in it." She took it out and held it up to Loretta. It was clear and slimy and completely unimpressive.

"So I wait a minute and blow on it a little, to, well, dry it out some."

Then she stuck her finger straight up, her maroon blazer straining at its shoulder seam. She looked like a woman cheering on her favorite football team.

"And I wait," she said, lifting her chin and going still.

There was a certainty that infected the woman's features when she closed her eyes. She was caught up in a waking dream that dealt with the nature of things, so Loretta waited with her, standing still in the dewy grass. She looked out over the lawn and saw her mother on the periphery, holding the dishcloth as if it were a talisman. Her back, for once, was to her home. Loretta's father was watching Timothy gesture at the men, hands in pockets, a gray hoodie pulled over his thin frame. Her parents were like two stars back in the beginning of things, racing as fast as they could to the opposite borders of their universe.

After ten minutes, the woman opened her wide eyes and smiled something shy at Loretta.

"It's going to be a great day for flying," she said.

They reached their ascent into the cloud and the world looked small and doll-like beneath them — tiny as bird bones, separated like puzzle pieces of green and brown and blue that mapped out a breakable world.

"When you get to where you don't know who you are, then something bad's happening to you," her father said.

He looked over the edge, a mixture of things on his face that Loretta couldn't recognize. She looked over too, eventually, peering into the haze of water particles that looked like insect wings. But they sparkled. There were vivid flashes of light that trembled all around them. Violin strings of atoms, tangled up in chemistry, ancient and complex, and pleasantly muddled. She breathed in deeper — that delicious vapor you could only find in the sky, in the upper regions of things.

"Dad, look."

They were passing through the cloud with remarkable speed, or maybe it was passing through them, but there they were, at least fifty other balloons bobbing like ships, turning, bounced by the atmosphere like toys in a child's bath. Every color was represented. Their own green and purple; a fire-lit orange that blazed against the blurry blue of sky; a deep black with gray, chicken-footed flecks; a pomegranate ruby that looked like the inside of a lover's mouth; a star-soaked blue, imperial and above the rest, its occupants four black dots, straining down to see what was below.

"We made it," she breathed, clutching his hand in hers, pressing it tight like a clam, warm fingers jumbled up in resolute love. *Inevitable, the inevitable*, her thoughts strummed through her mind.

Her father looked around him, his face unset and vulnerable for the first time in ages. "Yes, yes, Loretta. That we have."

ACKNOWLEDGEMENTS

FIRST AND FOREMOST, I want to thank my mother, Madora Sellers, for teaching me about books. She read to me as a child nightly, and always chose the most fantastic tales, like kings who hold court in the bathtub and nannies that fly. I grew up believing that it was my duty to read, and that the more I read, the closer I would come to meeting the characters and sharing bits and parts of their worlds. I also want to thank my father, Grant Sellers, for not freaking out about my literary plans. He never once suggested a more lucrative and steady career, but instead, realized I had a dream far too weighty to dismiss. And for that, I'm thankful. My grandfather, John McIntyre, taught me big words at the age of three, and I genuinely believe that kick-started my career as a word junkie. I got a better education from him than I did in school, and he taught me to love learning, instead of fear it. I also want to thank Tom Franklin, both my mentor and friend, for teaching me about writing in college. He is a kind teacher, but someone you don't want to disappoint, someone whose pride you seek. Beth Ann Fennelly, thank you so incredibly much for being a role model to me, and the best kind, really: a smart, independent, and wonderfully gracious woman. Mary Miller — many thanks, too. You were so kind to read my work, to encourage me. Adam Ray, Ben Zuerlein, Molly Harris, and Alex Kynerd: you guys read my work throughout college and commented with truthfulness, tact, and insight. Thank you. And to the rest of my friends who always, always supported me: you have no idea how much your optimism helped me. And finally, Kent Gustavson, my wonderful editor — thank you so incredibly much for taking a chance on these stories. Your willingness and enthusiasm have helped me so much, and encouraged their completion.

ABOUT THE AUTHOR

MARY B. SELLERS is a born and bred southerner. She graduated from The University of Mississippi in May of 2013, with a Bachelor's Degree in English. She is the Associate Publisher for Blooming Twig, as well as a freelance writer for several publications. She's had stories and essays published in Thought Catalog, *Deep South Magazine, Mississippi Magazine, Portico Magazine, Danse Macabre, Gingerbread House, Mouse Tales Press,* and ThatLitSite.com. She also writes book reviews at WhatIsThatBookAbout.com. Sellers now lives in Jackson, MS.

www.ingramcontent.com/pod-product-compliance
Lightning Source LLC
Chambersburg PA
CBHW070826250626
47170CB00006B/2219